THE ART OF KEEPING COOL

THE ART
OF KEEPING COOL

JANET TAYLOR LISLE

SCHOLASTIC INC.

New York   Toronto   London   Auckland   Sydney
Mexico City   New Delhi   Hong Kong   Buenos Aires

ISBN 0-439-32338-X

12 11 10 9 8 7 6 5   1 2 3 4 5 6/0

Printed in the U.S.A.   40

First Scholastic printing, October 2001

Book design by Ann Bobco
The text of this book is set in Centaur MT.

For Richard Jackson

THE ART OF KEEPING COOL

1

EARLY SATURDAY MORNING we heard the big guns were pulling close to Sachem's Head.

The word was they'd begin passing through town sometime between ten and eleven o'clock, so my cousin Elliot and I walked up Parson's Lane right after breakfast. We stood along the side of West Main Road with a raw sea wind whipping past our ears and it wasn't long before we got so cold we had to start hopping.

"Hey Robert, did we have to get here so early?" Elliot panted between hops.

"We had to," I panted back. "It's going to be history."

This was early in March 1942, barely three months after Pearl Harbor was bombed and America went to war against the Nazis and the Japanese, and we weren't the only ones on the road that morning. Soon people began to stream out from everywhere and wait at the ends of their driveways. Kids were climbing trees to look up the road. Every so often somebody would ride by in a car or on a bike and yell out a progress report. *They're at Wickham Road, won't be long now! They're up to Mrs. Grinnell's!*

They were mighty sixteen-inch bore naval guns, two of them—the largest and most powerful long-range weapons at that time. I'll never forget how the first tremendous body rose over the hill, its long, gray barrel pointed back up the road. An escort of armed soldiers walked soberly alongside.

"Stand back," I told Elliot. "It might speed up coming down."

There was no need to worry. Each gun was chained on two—not one but two—flatbed haulers because it was so huge, and the trucks that pulled the flatbeds were overwhelmed by their loads and inched forward with agonized groans and shudders, even going downhill.

A two-year-old child could have walked faster, someone said.

And done less damage to the road, someone else observed.

Across the way, I saw a tall, boney man in a blue cap take a notepad out of his knapsack and bend to write in it. I thought he was a reporter from one of the Providence newspapers, and felt proud to be there at such a momentous event.

The guns had been statewide news all week. They had already been two days on the road coming from the Riverton train depot, ten miles away, and would require another half day to haul to Fort Brooks. Along their route, a bridge had been reconstructed over an inlet to accommodate their weight. A yapping dog had darted too close and been crushed under one of the flatbed's slow-moving wheels. Marion Wainright, a local pacifist, had threatened to throw herself under another wheel. She was arrested and taken away to the police station to cool her heels. People weren't so tolerant of freethinkers back then, especially in a New England coastal village where the world hadn't yet shown much of a face.

These were not the first guns to be brought down the road. The fort complex—there were actually three batteries, each looking out to sea in a different direction—had been quietly accumulating artillery and soldiers for several months. But they were by far the largest weapons, the far-thest shooting, and not a sight to miss if you were inter-ested in the tools of war, as I was.

Most folks out that morning had heard a pretty close description of what they were going to see, and they still caught their breaths when the guns came over the hill. They edged away from the road as each gun's 143 tons and sixty-eight feet of molded steel rattled and clanked and cracked the macadam going by on the way to the job of protecting us, and the Rhode Island coast, from the Germans.

The war hadn't scared me yet and it didn't scare me that morning, I was glad to find out. My father was flying with the Royal Canadian Air Force out of England. He was one of the first Americans to go overseas. The country was gearing up, preparing to fight. I was impressed all right—"Elliot, look at those monsters!"—but I stood my ground as the guns rolled toward us down the hill, even when the earth began to rumble and shake under our feet. Turning, I saw my cousin Elliot's face empty of every emotion except terror.

"El, it's okay. They're not going to shoot."

Elliot had a problem—he registered things too deep. Sometimes it seemed to me as if his receivers were turned up too high on the world, and what he saw and heard came at him with extra force. These days, he mostly knows how to hide it. He's made it out and been around, picked up a name for himself, though like anybody, he can get caught off guard sometimes. He'll look too far or see too small and find himself on the verge of panic. But he's mastered the art of keeping cool and can put up a good defense so no one can tell.

Back in the spring of 1942, when we were both thirteen years old, Elliot Marks didn't have many defenses, and I could look in his eyes and see everything he was feeling.

"Really, you don't have to be scared."

"Who's scared?" Elliot lied, chewing deep into his hand. When he got nervous, he had a tic of biting into the L-shaped place between his thumb and his first finger. Not a hard bite, just a sort of rhythmic gnawing. He was no coward, though. That day he stayed with me, following the flatbeds down to where they turned in at the gate to the fort.

A private was on duty at the guardhouse and wouldn't let us through. We hung around looking for empty Coke bottles in the tall grass where the soldiers tossed them going by in their Jeeps. Six empties could get you five cents at the store in town. We didn't find any and, with nothing else doing at the fort, we set off for home, taking a back route along the beaches.

"I'm going to draw those guns as soon as I get home," Elliot said. Even then he could draw anything, just from looking at it once.

"I'm going to ask your dad if he can get us in to see them," I told him. "Their shells weigh a ton. A ton! Can you believe it?"

Elliot's father was a plumber and he had a government contract to work at the fort. It was the thing that was saving Elliot's parents, moneywise, that year.

"He can't get you in," Elliot said. "You can only get in for special stuff, like the movies."

"Well, somehow I'm getting in. Those guns can shoot twenty-six miles—that's over Martha's Vineyard."

"Mike Parini told me he saw a German sub," Elliot suddenly remembered.

"Where?"

"Off South Shore, toward the islands. Not the whole thing—the periscope coming up. But it was probably a lobster buoy or something."

"It might have been a sub," I said. "They're out there.

They torpedoed that tanker off Newport in January. You know they're looking for more hits. They'd invade us if they could. These guns are getting here just in time."

"These guns," Elliot said, shaking his head, "these guns are . . ." He stopped walking, and I saw his face go into the same freeze as when he'd first seen the long gray barrels come over the hill.

"Come on, El, don't do that."

Elliot started walking again, but he wouldn't talk. Except once he came to a halt and asked, "Hey Robert, did you see that guy?"

"What guy?"

"When the guns were coming, the big, skinny guy across the road in the blue cap? That was Abel Hoffman, the painter. He was famous over there."

"Over where? Abel who?" I asked, three times in a row. But Elliot had gone into another of his shut-downs and wouldn't answer. Low under his breath, I heard him mutter:

"I'm drawing them, that's what I'm doing. As soon as we're home, I'm getting them down."

2

THERE ARE PEOPLE in this world who are naturally open and easy to get to know, and there are difficult people, the ones who put up barricades and expect you to climb over them.

Elliot Marks was the second kind of person. The first time I saw him, he was standing outside without a coat on in the middle of a freezing New England February, mopping his nose and looking up into the bare limbs of a tree, staring up as if something amazing was there. Nothing was, or not that I could see anyway.

"Who is that?" I whispered to my mother.

We had just arrived at my Grandpa and Grandma Saunders' house in Rhode Island, a place we'd never visited before. My mother had brought me and my five-year-old sister, Carolyn, east from our farm in Ohio to stay in Sachem's Head while our father was away fighting. She'd been lonely by herself, and found it hard to keep the farm running with just me to help. When Grandma Saunders wrote to say a cottage had come empty next door on Parson's Lane, and why didn't she bring the children and live there, my mother went right out and bought our train tickets. It shocked me how fast she did it.

"What about Dad? He expects us to stay here," I protested.

"I'll write him. We'll get the post office to forward his letters until then," she answered.

"Who wants to live in a cottage when we already have a whole house?"

"It's on the ocean. There's a beach nearby. Carolyn will like that."

"But, what about the farm? Are you just going to let it go down?"

"I'll lease out the fields I can," she said. "I would've had to do that anyway. Where was I going to find hired help with every able-bodied man enlisted in the service?"

"Well, what about the hogs? You can't leave them!"

After we moved east, I used to wake up in the mornings with a picture in my mind of our old house, of how the fields spread out flat in all directions around it, and the sky streamed over it like a great river, sometimes deep and blue, sometimes muddy, stirred up, racing with clouds.

"There's wing room out here," my father used to say, dredging up an old term from his test pilot days. His eyes would look out across a field he'd just plowed, then come back to me squeezed in beside him on the tractor.

"Plenty of room to wag your wings when you need to," he'd say.

I'd never flown in an airplane but I liked the idea of having wing room. I liked being on my own, working by myself. I had friends but didn't have to be close-in with people every minute of the day. There was a kind of strength in knowing you could stand by yourself. My father had it, I knew that. It was what had brought him to Ohio in the first place, to buy land and start the farm. Now it was what had sent him over to England ahead of everybody else to fight the Nazis.

My father had a bad leg. He walked with a hitch in his stride, the result of a plane crash that had nearly killed him before he met my mom, he said. But he never let it stop him from doing what he wanted. He never talked about it or made excuses, and if his limp stood out in people's minds in the beginning, they'd forget it as they got to know him. That leg just didn't go with the rest of him. Most of the time, he seemed to forget it, too, because every once in a while he'd try to jump a brook or climb a ladder too fast and he'd fall. Afterwards, he'd pick himself up and go on without a word, even if he was hurt. From the look on his face, I'd know not to say anything either.

Of course, I knew my mother could stand alone, too. Her parents had died when she was a baby and she had to live with relatives growing up. She'd learned how to fight for herself by the time she met my father in Cincinnati. They planned out the farm together, built the house, cleared the fields. She'd worked right along with him, and cared as much, but:

"We'll sell the hogs . . . and the chickens," she answered me that day, so fast I could see she'd been thinking of something like this for a while. It was a month after the Japs bombed Pearl Harbor. My dad had been gone more than six months by then.

"That's the money we'll use for train fare," she said. "And for rent on this cottage your grandmother's found us. And for living on while I see about a job. I'm not planning to hang on your grandfather's coattails like everyone else back there."

"A job!" I snorted. "What kind of job?"

"There's a big torpedo factory in Newport that's hiring. Your Aunt Nan just started working there. She says I could, too."

"Aunt Nan, who's that?"

She glanced over at me. "Your father's sister. You know, Aunt Nan and Uncle Jake? They live there with your grandmother and grandfather in Sachem's Head. In the same house now, since Jake lost his business. It must be like Grand Central Station with all your grandfather's patients coming and going."

"What patients?"

"Robby! He's Dr. Saunders, the town doctor. Did you forget everything your father ever told you?"

He'd never told me anything, that was the trouble.

Vaguely, I'd heard of them though, names in holiday cards, on birthday gifts done up in fancy, Eastern wrap. I remembered my father laughing over a pair of fake red leather cowboy boots they sent me for my sixth or seventh birthday.

"What do they think, that he's about to start taking square dancing lessons?" he asked my mother.

From the tone he used, I knew all I needed to about those relatives in Rhode Island. Red-booted Easterners was how I began to think of them.

"This whole idea is stupid," I told Mom. "You've never even had a real job."

That insulted her. "I suppose I could learn," she snapped, "the same way I've been learning to run this entire farm by myself."

We left barely a month later. Three days on the train, sleeping berths at night. A crowd of servicemen was on board riding east with us, and there were many others—sailors, marines, airmen—in the stations we went through, waiting for connections, duffle bags slung over their shoulders. I watched them and edged up to listen to their talk when I could. They were headed to training camps in Maryland, Virginia, or North Carolina. From there they'd ship overseas to fight. They'd be in Europe by September, or on a battleship off Gibraltar. A lot of them wanted to get to the Pacific to give it to the Japs. The Germans were Krauts and they were going to get beat.

"My dad's over there right now, flying with the Royal

Canadian Air Force out of England. He's a pilot," I told them a few times. The response was always terrific.

"Hey, good man!"

"That-a-way!"

"How'd he get there so fast?"

"He used to fly for the mail service. Then he was a test pilot for the U. S. Army," I'd explain. "He knows a lot about the bombers President Roosevelt's sending over to help England, so he was asked to go."

"Hush, Robert, that's boasting," my mother would say. She didn't like talking about where my father was or what he might be doing. It was bad luck, she said, to harp on what you didn't know.

Uncle Jake was at the Providence train station to meet us when we came in late in the afternoon. He drove us in his plumber's pick-up down the coast to Sachem's Head, and we had just stepped down out of the truck into Grandma Saunders' welcoming hug, with Aunt Nan and Grandpa Saunders looking on behind, when:

"Who is that?" I asked about the coatless person standing back from everyone, shivering, mopping his nose and looking up of all places, up into a tree instead of down at the important thing that was happening: our arrival.

"You know who that is!" my mother whispered.

"No I don't."

"It's Elliot. Your cousin Elliot, Jake and Nan's son. He's younger than you, I think."

He was the same age as it turned out. Five months older, in fact, but smaller, shyer, standing back from everyone as if he was afraid to call attention to himself. It was this I first noticed about him, that no one tried to introduce Elliot to us. No one asked him what he was doing staring up into a tree. No one told him to go put on a coat. Slow was how I read him in the beginning. Slow and probably sickly.

"Hello," I said, going past.

"Oh, hello." Elliot brought his strange gaze down from the tree and applied it to me.

"I didn't know you . . ." I began, and stopped. I was going to say, "I didn't know you existed."

"That's all right, I didn't know about you either," Elliot said, getting the message anyway. "Until last week when they said you were coming. I guess our families didn't keep up too well."

"I guess not."

"Excuse me," Elliot said, glancing over my shoulder. He turned and walked away to a far edge of the yard where he began to beat his hands against the sides of his legs, to keep the blood flowing in them, most likely. Night was falling; the temperature outside couldn't have been more than fifteen degrees.

I looked around to see what had made him go off so fast. Grandpa Saunders was coming up. For a doctor, he was not very friendly-looking. He was tall, with a round, bald head and eyes that jumped out at you sharp and clear behind steel-rimmed glasses. A few minutes before, he'd shaken my hand and bent down stiffly to kiss my mother on her cheek. Now I saw him checking me over again.

"You've got the Callahan looks," he said, stopping beside me. "Your grandmother's side of the family, not mine."

"My mother thinks I look like my father," I told him. He didn't answer, just gave a kind of grunt and looked over toward Elliot.

"That fool is going to catch his death out here," he said. "Would you be standing outside in this weather without a coat, waving your arms around like some Godforsaken windmill?"

"Not usually," I said carefully. I knew a rigged question when I heard one.

"Not usually, not usually," Grandpa Saunders muttered. He turned his back and marched off toward the house.

We were all invited inside to dinner. Grandma Saunders had been in the kitchen since breakfast, readying up for our arrival. She had quick, dark eyes and was always reaching out to pat your shoulder or squeeze your hand when she talked. I liked her. I wondered why my father had barely mentioned her over the years, and never wanted to visit.

"Nobody cooks like your grandma," Aunt Nan told me on the way inside. "She's been wanting to get her hands on you and Carolyn for years."

"Why didn't Dad ever bring us here?"

"Oh, various complications," Aunt Nan said, lightly. I

saw her eyes meet my mother's over my head. Something about the word "complications" made me think of my father's lameness, and I wondered if travel used to be harder for him than it was now.

"It's about time these children met the rest of their family. We're glad to be here, having dinner with you at last," my mother said, too gladly, I thought, considering all we'd left behind.

"I feel sick!" Carolyn announced then. "We just ate on the train and I'm going to throw up all over the place if I have to eat again."

Mom and I looked at each other because Carolyn always felt sick whenever she got to someplace she wasn't sure about. If you didn't watch out, she could make herself sick, too.

"You come with me, young lady," Mom said, and snatched her off to one side. They went to find the room we'd be staying in that night, until we moved to our own cottage down the road the next morning.

I followed everyone into a small dining room where a long wooden table was set for dinner and sat down across from . . . Elliot, was it? We glanced at each other under cover of the conversation. He was sitting very straight, his spine jammed back against the chair, which was itself set back from the table a bit. I had the strange impression he was trying to disappear.

Grandpa Saunders took up a position at the head of the

table, carving fork in one hand, carving knife in the other, a glistening brown roast chicken on a platter in front. Plates were passed down to him, one by one, for slices of meat, then sent over to Grandma, who served up peas, mashed potatoes, and hot rolls.

"Everything's homegrown," she said proudly when my mother came back with Carolyn. "Except the rolls, of course. They're plain home-baked."

Everyone laughed politely, except Elliot. He was staring up again, at the ceiling this time.

"I put up a whole larder of vegetables at the farm last fall, but they're going to have to wait till we get back," my mother said. "To tell the truth, I'm not missing them much."

"Would you like dark meat or light, sonny?" Grandpa called when my turn came to pass up a plate.

"Dark, I guess," I said. I like white meat better but didn't want to sound puny.

"You can't guess about what you like or don't like, sonny. You've got to know!" Grandpa shouted, waving his knife in the air. "Is it light or dark?"

"Dark!" I shouted back.

Grandpa forked a huge chicken leg onto my plate.

"I understand you and your mother didn't have too much luck trying to run that hog farm out there by yourselves," he said, passing the plate over to Grandma. "Bit off a little more than you could chew, is that right?"

"Not really," I said. "We were doing okay. We just couldn't get hired help because of everybody going into the service like Dad, otherwise we would have—"

"That's what I said!" Grandpa roared. He cut me off so fast I was embarrassed and felt the blood come up in my face.

Across the table, Elliot was having white meat and watching me from under his lids. He was still in that ridiculous straight-backed position. When Aunt Nan asked if he wanted more milk, he said:

"Yes please, Mother, if I could," in a voice that would have been about right for a fancy dinner party in New York.

Then he did something even stranger. He reached across the space between him and the table, took up his knife and fork and, at arm's length, began to cut up his chicken. It looked almost impossible to do, but finally he had a little mound of pieces and started to eat. He'd spear a chicken piece with the tip of his fork and whip it back to his mouth as if he were a bullfrog snapping up a fly.

"What sports do you play?" I asked him after a while.

"I don't play sports," Elliot said. "My knees go out."

"I played football at school this year," I told him. "And a bunch of us play ice hockey in the winter. There's a pond on our farm."

"Ohio has ice in the winter?" Elliot asked. "I thought it was too far south. Doesn't the Mississippi River run through there?"

This was so amazingly stupid I didn't know what to say. Any map could tell you where Ohio was, and that the Mississippi wasn't just a southern river. It flowed through the north, too. It *started* in the north, for God's sake! I dug into my mashed potatoes and didn't look over at Elliot again.

But while the dishes were being washed in the kitchen and I was roaming around trying to keep clear of Grandpa Saunders, who was on a couch in the front parlor rattling through a newspaper, Elliot appeared suddenly at my side. He asked if I wanted to come up and see his room.

"I could show you something," he said, taking a large bite of his hand.

"Well, all right," I agreed, not very enthusiastically.

The room was up a flight of stairs at the back of the house. It was an attic, really, with a bare light bulb hanging down from the rafters, old floor lamps, wicker chairs, and traveling trunks piled in dusty gloom at the far end. Elliot had one of those fold-up cots for a bed, and a chair, and a table which when I came in had nothing on it but a pad of paper.

"I thought you might want to see this . . . um . . . picture," he said, looking sideways at the pad.

"Okay," I said, and walked across to look.

"It's stupid, I know," Elliot said, backing away and blinking fast. He was about the most nervous person I'd ever met.

It was a drawing done with a plain lead pencil.

"Did you do this?" I asked. It looked too good for a kid, like something a real artist might draw.

There was Grandpa Saunders with the carving knife raised and his eyes pointy and dangerous behind his spectacles, exactly the way he'd looked bellowing down the dinner table at me. Everything from the angry bulge between his eyebrows to the pattern of white dots on his bow-tie was drawn in. The salt and pepper shakers were in front of him and the bowl of gravy. Grandma's roast chicken was there, hunched down on the platter as if it were trying to take cover, too. It made me laugh a little.

"Did you draw it, really?"

"Yes."

"But when? We just finished dinner."

"A little while ago. Do you like it?"

"Well, yes," I said. "But how did you do it?"

"I don't know, I just did. Do you see what it says underneath?"

Elliot pointed to a line of block lettering written in at the bottom of the drawing. It read, "Bit off more than you could chew, is that right, sonny?"

I burst out laughing. I couldn't help it. Elliot stood by with a cautious smile.

"I'm glad you like it."

"I don't know why it's so funny, but it is."

"It's because he made you feel so bad. You have to watch out. He does that."

"I was hoping no one had noticed."

"Don't worry, no one did," Elliot said. "Except me."

Right then was when I realized how I'd underestimated this strange cousin. I shook my head and laughed some more. And Elliot gave a somewhat brighter smile, but warily, as if he wasn't sure he was allowed to.

"I'm sorry I said that crazy thing about the Mississippi River," he said. "I get kind of worried about stuff at the table. Tell me about your farm. It sounds like a pretty good place."

So I sat down and told him how I was going to miss the spring planting out there that year, but I guessed it would get done by somebody. I explained how we grew corn mostly, plus some other crops like wheat, and how hogs and corn sort of go together on a farm, because the hogs get fat eating the corn and then you can sell them for a good price and buy land to plant more corn.

"My dad worked our farm up from nothing," I boasted. "Well, my mother did a lot, too."

"Sounds like things were going great out there until your father had to leave," Elliot said.

"They were," I said. "We were all real happy."

"Too bad my parents couldn't've gone out to stay with you instead of your mother coming here. Then we all could've worked together and you probably could have stayed," Elliot said. He wasn't saying it just to be nice, I could tell. He really wished it had happened.

After a while, neither of us felt like talking anymore. I said I ought to go help my mother carry in a few things from the truck for the night.

"Can I have the drawing?" I asked. "I'll keep it private, don't worry."

"Oh, it's for you," Elliot said. "That's why I drew it."

I folded up the sheet of paper and slid it into my back pocket, where just having it made the edges of my mouth twitch again when later that night, I saw Grandpa coming across the dim dining room on his way to bed.

"Who is that?" he roared out rudely.

"It's Robert," I said.

In the shadows, I saw his mouth close up and tighten. We met and passed without another word.

3

NOT ALL AT once after this, but by slow degrees, I began to get to know Elliot and understand the different parts of him. He wasn't a bad person overall, but he could be a real pain in the neck.

For one thing, he was slower than midnight and took forever to get places. I always had to stand around and wait for him to leave or come or get ready to do something. Sometimes, he wouldn't show up at all. He'd never apologize either. Usually I'd find him back in his room. He'd look up from whatever he'd gotten sidetracked on and say: "Oh, I guess I forgot," as if it wasn't his fault but just how things had naturally worked out.

Elliot didn't mean to be annoying. It turned out he had another sense of order. He'd worry frantically over tiny things that made no difference to anyone else: cups with cracks in them, lost buttons, little dead things like birds or squirrels that were hit on the road. He'd have to stop and bury them, no matter what. He'd rescue worms, too, if they were crawling into the road after a rainstorm, and put them back in the ditch they came out of. Whoever was with him had to stand around and wait. It didn't matter how mad you got.

In Elliot's mind, everyone and everything had to be where they were supposed to be, act the way they were supposed to act. If they didn't, he'd have to stop and put them right, which was pretty strange considering that Elliot himself wasn't exactly dependable.

He would promise to do a thing and then, when it was found out he hadn't done it, tell the biggest lies to cover up. Anyone would know he was lying, too, because he was so bad at it.

"Why don't you just say you forgot?" I asked him one time. "People wouldn't mind that much and it would make things more, you know, honest."

"Because I don't forget," Elliot said. In this case, he'd promised to stop on his way home from school and mail a letter my mother had given me for my father. I had to stay late to see a teacher. A couple of days afterwards, I found the letter sticking out of a book in his room.

"The post office was closed when I went," Elliot told me. "I was going to go back."

"Well, you could have put it in the post box out front. The post box is always open."

"It was locked," Elliot lied. "Don't ask me why, it's never happened before, but it was locked up tight."

Another maddening thing was his fake manners with grown-ups. I couldn't stand all the 'pleases' and 'thank yous' he was always pouring on with them, or the way he'd get out of doing chores by making Grandma feel guilty. He'd pretend he wasn't feeling well, or that his knees were bothering him, some little thing. Then she'd ask me if I minded doing his jobs for him, which I did but what could I say?

Nothing was ever really wrong with Elliot that I could see. He acted strange, that was all. He had a way of squinting, then opening his eyes wide, then squinting again that made people stare at him.

"Were you sick before I came?" I asked him once. His skin was so pale. Sometimes it looked green, as if it was growing mold.

"I don't think so," Elliot said.

"You would know if you were sick," I said, feeling a little like Grandpa Saunders on an attack.

"You wouldn't know if you were too sick to know you were."

"Are you saying you were too sick to know it?"

"Did I say that?"

"Well, did you?"

"Did I what?"

"You know!"

A few more conversations like this and you were ready to strangle him.

No one in his house seemed to worry about Elliot, though. Or, if they worried, they'd long ago given up trying to do anything about it. Grandma hugged him and shook her head. Uncle Jake looked the other way, as if Elliot were some sort of riddle he couldn't guess the answer to. Aunt Nan cared about him a lot, but she was mostly away at work by the time I knew him, and didn't have time to keep up with him. You could see how money was a trouble to her and Uncle Jake. They were both working like mad to hold up their end.

Grandpa, of course, would hardly look at Elliot. He thought he was an idiot and a weakling, I'd seen that the first day. There wasn't much that Grandpa hated more than idiots and weaklings.

Sometimes it seemed as if Elliot was a sort of ghost in his own family, he went so quietly and unnoticeably around the house. Even his amazing talent had to be a secret, though why anyone who could draw that well would be hiding it, instead of getting up honestly and making something of it, I couldn't understand. But no one ever talked about it, and:

"Don't show them! Don't tell. They don't want to know!" Elliot would say whenever he showed me some new picture he'd done. This was pretty often because, as I began to realize in the weeks after our move to Sachem's Head, Elliot drew all the time. He couldn't stop.

He drew in the mornings before breakfast, at school

during classes, at night while he was supposed to be doing his studies. He kept scraps of paper and a pencil in his pocket, ready to sketch whatever came along—the three-legged dog that hung around the playground, witchy old Miss Wilson teaching algebra.

He didn't keep the sketches or show them to anyone except me. He'd throw them away almost as soon as they were done.

"Don't you want this?" I'd ask. "It's so good."

He'd shrug. "What for? I don't need it anymore."

His memory was so sharp for the lines of what was around him that he could come home and draw a face, a room at school, whole trees, branch for branch, that he'd passed along the road. It was as if a little camera was inside his head, and everything he looked at was snapped and stored away. Later, he could choose the pictures he wanted to bring out and put down. Except, what he mostly chose wasn't anything beautiful or wondrous, like what usually gets drawn. It would be something funny that we could laugh about, or that bothered him somehow, like the big guns coming down the road.

Half an hour after we got home that March afternoon, Elliot had already finished a pencil drawing of them: the huge gray barrels, the crowd of people watching, toothpicks by comparison.

I thought it was great. "Everything was just like that," I told him, "only this is even a little better. I'm much scareder looking at this picture than I was on the road."

"That's what happens," Elliot answered with a nod. "If I do it right, that's exactly what happens. The real thing gets caught."

"Caught?" I didn't understand.

"It can't get you," Elliot explained. "You've got it, down on paper."

The arrival of the big guns began to change things in Sachem's Head. People became more anxious. They saw how the Germans really might be cooking up something, an espionage mission or an invasion. The fort had been quite relaxed about security up to then, and easygoing with folks in town. Now it stiffened up. A civilian couldn't get in the gates without a written pass. Even Uncle Jake couldn't get in without one. I knew it was hopeless to ask him to get me in so I didn't even try.

Elliot and I began to see all kinds of high-ranking officers, captains and majors and such, riding around in military Jeeps. We had a book that we studied all the time which told how to recognize insignias and decorations on soldiers' uniforms. We weren't the only ones who had it. A lot of kids had this book. Everyone was always trying to outdo everyone else in spotting the highest rank. It was a big event of the whole day if you saw somebody important. Mike Parini said he saw a general once, but no one believed him. He wasn't a liar or anything. If you knew Mike, you knew he had this kind of hopeful imagination that saw things it wanted to see.

Meanwhile, news about the war was pouring in from all sides and we were all following the newspapers and the radio to find out what was happening. Things were heating up in the Pacific. After Pearl Harbor, the Japs thought they had us down and they invaded the Philippines, the island of Guam and some other South Sea islands. There wasn't much we could do about it. Grandpa got disgusted with General MacArthur for getting trapped at Corregidor. Then he got disgusted with Roosevelt for not sending MacArthur enough troops to fight his way out. We'd hear about it every night at dinner, loud and clear.

We already knew how the Germans had invaded all of Europe, and how they were bombing England to pieces, which was pretty frightening when I thought about my father being there. Sometime in April, reports began to come in of German U-boats, submarines that is, being sighted off our coast. Then a U. S. convoy ship was sunk up near Maine and people got worried. Mike Parini saw two more periscopes rise out of the ocean. This time he wasn't the only one.

Everyone started reporting them, and even Elliot and I couldn't look out to sea without some flickery movement there making us jump. Mostly it wasn't anything but a wave or a bunch of seagulls floating together, but sometimes we weren't sure. That was the problem. Suddenly you couldn't be sure. No one knew what the Germans were thinking or what they might be planning. If they were crazy enough to be invading everywhere else, why not here, too?

Elliot and I were pretty much spending all our time together by then. May came. The days got milder and the cold winds that drove in off the sea began to let up. It was still cold, though. That year it seemed as if summer would never come.

"When can we go to the beach?" Carolyn was always asking my mother. "You promised we'd go swimming at the beach." She was too little to care anything about the war. Periscopes coming up out at sea didn't faze her one bit.

"Can't we get you interested in anything but the beach?" my mother would say. She wasn't too excited about Carolyn playing down there, even if it did get warm, with all that was going on.

"No you can't! You can't!" Carolyn would scream. Little kids have a one-track mind when they've decided on something they want.

We'd been in our rented cottage for three months by then. It was rough and plain, but we liked it all right. There was no telephone or radio, like we'd had at the farm, but Mom said we'd get them as soon as we could. She'd found a good job at the Naval Torpedo Station in nearby Newport.

"I'm learning to spot weld," she said. "They needed welders so I signed up. Why not? It pays double and it's no harder than making buttonholes."

It was pretty funny to think of my mother manning a

blow torch, walking around in workmen's overalls making torpedoes. I kept my mouth shut though. I could see how seriously she took it.

"Don't bring it up with your grandparents," she told me. "They've got old-fashioned views of where women belong. It's bad enough that Nan and I are out working for wages at all."

Gasoline was expensive—soon it would be rationed for the war—so she and Aunt Nan drove to Newport with some other women every weekday morning, leaving Carolyn with Grandma Saunders. Since they usually didn't get back till after seven at night, I had my suppers with Elliot and did my homework in Elliot's attic room.

I'd entered the local school in Elliot's seventh grade class, and gotten to know a lot of other kids. I didn't spend much time with them, though. Elliot, being the odd kind of goose he was, hadn't made many friends over the years, and in fact was down to really none when I got there. So I hung around with him. I didn't mind. We'd hook up at the end of the school day and walk home, talking or not talking, depending on how Elliot was feeling about things.

It was on one these walks that Elliot introduced me to the man he'd told me about on the day of the big guns, the tall man in the blue cap whose name was Abel Hoffman. Maybe "introduce" is the wrong word, because Elliot no sooner saw him coming up the road, than he jumped into the bushes and dragged me in after.

"Elliot! What's the matter with you?"

"It's him, Mr. Hoffman! Don't let him see me."

"But why?" I peered down the road. The man in the blue cap hadn't noticed us yet. He was walking slowly, staring into a field he was passing. He wore foreign-looking, dark leather boots that laced high up his shins, and had a walking stick that he swung forward and touched to the ground every few steps.

"I can't speak to him!" Elliot whispered. "He's in a book."

"In a book! I thought you said he was a painter." I tried to stand up but Elliot yanked me back down.

"He is a painter. That's why he's in the book."

"Well, I'm getting up."

"No! No!"

"I'm getting up and you are, too . . ."

"No!"

"Because if he's a painter you should meet him," I said. Elliot was terrible about meeting people. That was one of the reasons he didn't have any friends.

"But I have met him," Elliot cried in a sort of wail. I was already pulling him out of the brush, though. I got him back on the road just in time for Abel Hoffman to more or less run right into us.

"Ah! Pardon!" He stopped in his tracks. He had a knapsack on his back with a lot of rags and paintbrushes sticking out of it. Some kind of a collapsible stool was tied to the back. You could see he'd probably been out painting somewhere.

"So, you!" he said to Elliot. He seemed pretty happy about running into him. "But how are you? How is your hart? You are never coming to see me."

Elliot looked off nervously into the distance and tried some fake manners.

"Well, hello Mr. Hoffman, so nice to see you again. This is my cousin Robert from Ohio. We've been really busy and I didn't have time to . . ."

Abel Hoffman put out his hand to me and dipped his shoulders, very polite and courtly. He was tall and really thin. His clothes flapped around whenever he moved. Under his pants, his legs looked like sticks.

"I am most very pleased," he said, and shook my hand. "Do you also do hart, like your couchen. Er, I mean your . . . cowzen? Well, I mean like . . . this one here?"

He pointed at Elliot. His English was pretty bad. I could just barely understand him.

"Hart?"

"He means art," Elliot murmured, sounding half strangled.

"Oh art. No, not me. I can't draw at all."

"Well, well, too bad." Abel Hoffman lowered his head as if he was actually sorry to hear this, then he glanced at Elliot.

"So, now, we meet again. You are coming one day to see me, yah?"

Elliot didn't answer. He was chewing wildly on his hand. The painter looked at him and nodded.

"Is okay. Do not bring your har . . . your art. Another time, you bring. This time, you see what I do! I work and work to paint the ocean!" He gestured proudly toward Sachem's Head Point.

"The ocean!" Elliot echoed, as if he couldn't believe it.

"Yah, yah, come and look. Some afternoon, next week, after school. You know where? In my little studio?"

Elliot nodded unhappily.

"Good-bye, then. Cheerio, till we meet!"

He marched off in time to his walking stick, looking like some kind of crazy insect flicking along. When he'd gone a little way, he turned back with a shout.

"Pardon! You bring also this . . . this . . . your cousin!" he cried triumphantly to Elliot, conquering the word at last. He made his funny bow and went off again.

Elliot was in such a gnawing, nervous state after this that I hardly dared look at him. We walked very fast down the road without speaking. After a few minutes, he seemed to be getting back in charge of himself, so I asked:

"When did you meet him before?"

"Last summer at the town fair."

"And?"

"And what?"

"What happened?"

At first he wouldn't say. Finally he gave in and told me how he'd come across the painter drawing portraits of people for money. Two dollars for a pencil drawing, four for pastel.

"I'd never seen anybody work with pastels, so I watched him," Elliot said. "Some other kids were watching, too, and Mr. Hoffman was really nice about it. He set us up with a few of his pastel crayons, and paper, and told us we could draw whatever we wanted. It was just for fun, but afterwards he invited me to come to his house and bring other things I'd done."

"He liked your drawing."

"He didn't say that."

"He did, though. That's why he invited you. Did you go?"

"I was going to. Not to show anything, I would have died before that. I wanted to try his pastels again." Elliot paused. "Then I found out who he was."

"Who is he?"

"I told you! He's Abel Hoffman, the famous painter. And you better not tell anyone. And don't tell anyone he talked to us, either, especially not in this house." We were coming up on Grandma Saunders' kitchen door.

"Why not?"

"They don't like him."

"Why? He seems like a good person."

"He is," Elliot said. "But they'll be mad. He's a German, you know, and people don't like that."

"A German!" A kind of freeze went through me. I'd seen he was a foreigner because of his accent, but I hadn't thought what kind.

"He's been living down in the woods since last spring.

Everyone knows he's there. I'm supposed to stay away from him."

There was no more time to talk just then. Grandma was in the kitchen with Carolyn getting supper started. We had to start doing chores. We carried coal up from the cellar for the stove, brought laundry in from the line, and swept off the back porch, which still had leaves on it from last fall. Not till after supper could we get away to Elliot's room.

As soon as we'd shut the door, Elliot went over and pulled a cardboard box out from under his bed. It was where he stored the important things he owned, including a crazy collection of wild birds' eggs that he kept in a bunch of old egg cartons. Usually, he'd have to stop and mull over his eggs, but now he was after something so he moved them aside. He took out a big, flat book from the bottom of the box.

"Here it is, the book Abel Hoffman's in. Your father gave it to me for my birthday last year."

"My dad?" I was amazed. "Does he usually give you birthday presents?"

"Not usually," Elliot said. "Just when we moved here with Grandma and Grandpa. I guess my mother must have told him we had to move. He didn't want her to, I know. They never talked much on the phone, but they talked about that."

We sat on the floor, our backs against the bed.

The book was called "Art in the Twentieth Century." Each chapter was about a different country in the world, with nice, color photographs of artworks and the artists who had done them. There were chapters on France and Italy, on Spain and Mexico, the United States and so on.

Abel Hoffman came up near the end of the chapter on Germany. There was even a black and white photo of one of his paintings, which was dark and wild and looked like a bunch of thorn bushes whipping around. A smaller photo was of him—or what he used to look like. He was a lot fatter when he was younger.

"His name was on a sign at the fair," Elliot said. "It sounded kind of familiar but I didn't think anything at first."

"Who would?" I said. "The artists at fairs aren't usually in books."

"A lot of people were mad that he dared to come and set up like that in the middle of town. Almost nobody asked him to draw them. Finally some out-of-town guys came and sat for him, but they wouldn't pay when he finished. They made fun of his English and said he was a fake because he didn't do real portraits but sort of impressions of people. He was really nice the whole time. People came and watched him work but they wouldn't talk to him. They just thought, 'Oh! A German!', and stared."

"Well, we are fighting a war against them. How did you figure out it was him?"

"I don't know. I'd been reading this book and suddenly I remembered, I guess. I looked him up and there he was."

"It's so strange."

Even stranger was to read:

> Abel Hoffman (1891–   ): One of the boldest of the new wave of modernist German painters and abstract expressionists. Since his first exhibitions in the early 1920s, his unusually personal, highly emotional work has exerted an ever-increasing influence on a younger generation of painters. Hoffman grew up outside Berlin, the son of a factory worker. In 1924, after a period of study at the Stadtische Kunstschule (Municipal Art School) in Frankfurt, he set up his own studio and immediately became the center of an important group of young modern painters.

"I don't get it," I said, when I'd finished reading the article. "Why is he over here?"

Elliot shook his head. "I guess he came before the war started and couldn't get back."

"Well, what's he doing way out here by himself in Sachem's Head where no one knows who he is? He should be in New York or some big city showing his paintings at museums if he's so good."

"I guess he should," Elliot said, "but he's not famous

here. I suppose he's just waiting around for the war to end so he can go home."

"I wonder what he thinks about the war," I said. "He must be pretty mad we're fighting his country."

"He probably doesn't think about it that way."

"Maybe he does," I said. "Maybe he hides things. Let's ask him a few questions when we go see him next week. You know, he really could be a spy over here on a mission."

"He's not a spy, and we're not asking him any questions because we're not going," Elliot said. He looked upset.

"Elliot, why?"

"No!"

"You're too scared?"

"It's not that."

"But he thinks you're good."

"He thinks I'm what I am. Someone who can draw a little. That's it. That's really all I can do."

"He probably has real paint."

"What do you mean, 'real paint'?"

"Paint!" I said. "He said he was painting the ocean, re- member? What would happen if Abel Hoffman let you borrow his paint? Have you ever tried real painting with a brush? I bet you haven't."

Elliot fell into a long silence after this. At last he said, "I don't know," in a hollow-sounding voice. His eyes narrowed, then widened, then narrowed again while the thought of painting rattled through his brain. They narrowed and widened again. And again.

"Elliot, don't do that," I said, but it was too late. His tic was taking over.

"Please stop that! Stop! "

There was no getting through to him. There never was when he went into one of his nervous shut-downs. He couldn't help himself any more than anyone could help him, either, so it was a matter of just waiting it out. When my mother called from downstairs that she was back from Newport and ready to go home, I got up from the floor and looked down at him.

"Hey El, do you mind if I borrow this book?" I asked him. "Just for tonight. I'll bring it back in the morning."

Elliot didn't answer, so I took it home.

4

ELLIOT WASN'T THE only ghost in Grandpa and Grandma Saunders' house. There was another one, a person so erased and invisible that I almost forgot about him myself when I was there.

This ghost had left no evidence of himself behind, though he'd grown up in that house and known the people who lived in it now. There was no memory of which room had been his, where he'd sat at the table, how he'd spent his time or which friends he'd brought home for dinner.

No one ever talked about the sports he played, though I knew for a fact he'd played football and ice skated, because I'd heard stories about this back in Ohio. No one ever said what kind of marks he'd got at school, though he must have gone to the same school I was in now.

Sometimes, in the middle of a class, I'd think: *I could be sitting at his desk!* I'd raise the wooden lid and look on the back where kids from the old days had carved their initials. There must have been a hundred initials carved there, but I never found my father's.

When we'd walk home from school I'd suddenly start wondering: *Did he walk home this same way?* It was strange to think of being in the footsteps of someone who'd left so long ago, who maybe didn't even know yet that his son was here, living in Sachem's Head, looking into his past.

"Why doesn't anyone ever want to talk about Dad?" I asked my mother a few weeks after we arrived. "Whenever I say anything, everybody looks upset."

"They're worried about him, I suppose," my mother said.

"But there's nothing of his around the house," I told her. "No one will say what room he had. I wanted to see his old bed, but Aunt Nan said they don't have it anymore."

"I'm not surprised," my mother said. "It's been a long time since your father was here."

I let the subject drop that time. I knew my mother worried a lot about my father. I didn't want to bother her any more. But another time I said:

"Grandma has pictures out around the house of Aunt Nan when she was little, but none of Dad. When I asked her where they were, she said she keeps them in a special place."

"Then I guess she does."

"But doesn't that seem strange? Why doesn't she put them where everyone can see them? Isn't she proud of what he's doing?"

My mother turned on me angrily then. "Of course she's proud! He's her son, after all. If Grandma chooses not to have his pictures about, that's her business. And please don't ask her any more about it. She's as worried as all of us and doesn't need a lot of rude poking and prodding to prove it."

That set me straight fast. I was sorry I'd ever brought the subject up. From then on, I didn't talk about Dad. I still wondered about him though, and kept my eyes and ears open around the house for stray pieces of information that might solve the puzzle.

Elliot's book was one of these stray pieces, and back in my room that night, I examined it closely. Not for more information on Abel Hoffman. The German artist was interesting, worth a deeper investigation, but he could wait. I opened to the book's inside cover and read the short inscription I'd caught sight of in Elliot's room that night. It was written in my father's handwriting.

> To Elliot, with hopes that this book will present new views and encourage you to travel far in pursuit of your goals. Happy Birthday, Kenneth B. Saunders (Uncle Ken).

It made me kind of jealous to read that. The thing was, my father never wrote to me from England. Even if I wrote to him, he'd always write back to my mother, with the idea that she'd pass his letters along to Carolyn and me afterwards. I missed hearing from him directly. I knew he was busy, probably thinking of me and wanting to see me, but I wished he'd write anyway so I could be sure. When I saw those private words he'd written to Elliot, I felt sort of depressed. It didn't matter that they'd been written more than a year ago, before he left for England.

Of course, my dad had given me plenty of books over the years. They were the kind of present he liked to give. He loved them himself, and would read for hours in the evenings at the farm, or on days when the weather forced him in. But I wondered why he'd sent Elliot this art book if he'd never given him anything before. As far as I knew, he'd never been interested in Elliot up till then. He'd certainly never talked about him. What had made him get so interested all of a sudden?

I examined the book's back cover and thumbed through the pages hoping for more evidence. There was none, so I laid it on the floor by my bed. I turned out the light, but I couldn't sleep. I began to think about the farm. My old homesick ache came back and I wished I was there again.

I imagined tall green walls of corn growing up in front of me, the Ohio sky sweeping over my head. I saw the hogs come leaping like clowns out of the barn (our hogs always had a great sense of humor) toward the outdoor pen where they lived in warm weather.

I saw my mother hanging up fresh wash and my sister throwing handfuls of straw at the barnyard rooster, who hated to be teased and flew at her with angry squawks that made her scream and laugh.

I looked for my father and at first he wasn't there. But then, high up in the sky of my mind, I found a small, silver airplane and watched as it flew toward me. Closer it came, closer and closer, until the drumming of the engine rose in my ear and I could almost see the pilot at the controls.

Almost but not quite. The shape was there but I couldn't make out the face. Would I recognize my own father in his flying gear? That was a question I'd been asking myself. I'd seen magazine photos of British RAF pilots in leather helmets and padded flight suits. It was cold up there in the air, my father had written this in one of his letters. "Colder than a freezer box. Even my eyelashes froze," he wrote.

I wanted this pilot to turn around so I could see his face. I waited and waited, staring at the shadowy head. I willed it to turn, sent my thought waves out there to tell it to turn, but it didn't, or wouldn't, and at last I gave up and drifted away into a sad kind of sleep.

The next morning there was bad news. Elliot and I heard it first thing at school from Grace Cody, whose family rented rooms to an officer from the fort.

"A ship got torpedoed by the Germans yesterday and sunk right off here," she was telling everyone.

"Off where?" I asked.

"I don't know, but close. The fort's been put in a state of readiness. The principal's going to make an announcement."

"What happens when you're in a state of readiness?" Elliot asked in a nervous voice.

"You're ready to shoot, of course," I told him. "If anything else happens, that's it, we shoot."

That made him look even jumpier and I was sorry I'd said it. Elliot didn't like guns. I used to wonder if he'd had a run-in with one when he was younger.

A student assembly was called in the lunchroom after lunch. The principal told us what had happened.

A six-thousand-ton British freighter carrying supplies to England had been sunk, torpedoed by a German submarine just south of Cape Cod. Eighteen crewmen were lost. Fifty-two survivors were rescued at sea, many taken to a town not far up the coast from Sachem's Head. Shocking as all this was, there was no immediate threat. Nothing to worry about, the principal said. The fort was monitoring the situation, reconnaissance planes were out patrolling the area.

"The most patriotic thing we can do is return to our classes and concentrate on our studies," he informed us. Everyone in the lunchroom groaned out loud.

"The trouble with patriotism is it gets used as an excuse for everything," Elliot complained to me that afternoon when we walked home. "Suddenly it's my patriotic duty to take out the trash and my patriotic duty to hang up the laundry."

"Well, otherwise you don't do anything," I pointed out. "I'm the one who has to help Grandma all the time, while you're lying around your room."

"I'm not lying around, I'm working," Elliot said.

"While I'm peeling potatoes."

"Tell Grandma you resign from duty. Say you've got homework. She always lets me off for that."

"She's afraid you're flunking out, that's why."

"I am flunking out," Elliot said with a shrug. He was hopeless about school. He didn't even pretend to care.

"Let's walk down to the fort," I said. "Then no one will have to be patriotic and maybe we can see what's going on."

"We know what's going on. They're in readiness," Elliot said.

"I know that! The point is, what kind of readiness. Come on, El, you'll see some great stuff for drawings."

"The fort is not my idea of good material."

It took a little more badgering, but finally he agreed to go.

The fort was at least two miles down the road. At that time, though Elliot had a bicycle, I didn't, so we walked everywhere. It took longer, but we could cut across fields or through shrub forests off the paved road. Elliot liked this because he could look for more wild birds' eggs. I never knew what it was about birds' eggs that got him so excited. He used to spend hours hunting for them. Woodcock eggs, plover eggs, sanderling eggs, seagull eggs, on and on. I began to look for them, too, just from being with him all the time. Once you start looking for almost invisible things like wild eggs, it's hard to stop.

Bushwhacking and egg-hunting this way, we got to the fort's front gates at about four o'clock. They were closed. A private was on duty, tipped back in a chair against the cement guard house, reading a magazine. All we could see beyond him was some movement far off that might have been trucks unloading something.

"Nothing looks any readier than usual," Elliot sniffed.

"Let's wait," I said. We sat down across the road.

A quarter of an hour went by, then an officer came out on foot, walking toward the guard, who jumped up and saluted. They had a short talk, more salutes, and the officer turned and walked back inside.

"That was a lieutenant colonel!" I whispered.

"How could you tell?"

"He had silver oak leaves on his shoulder."

Elliot was impressed. It was the first lieutenant colonel we'd ever seen.

"We've got to get in," I said. "How about if we circle around? Is there a way we could cut in off the road and get closer?"

"We could come up from the bay beach side," Elliot said, "but they probably have guards there, too."

"Let's try," I whispered. "Maybe we could see what they're doing with the big guns."

Elliot was not particularly in favor of this, but he followed me down the road. Around the bend, out of sight of the guard, we cut inland through dense thickets of brush and swamp maple. The ground was soft from recent rain and thaw, and our shoes got heavy with muck. After about

twenty minutes, we still hadn't come out on the beach. Elliot began to make noises about going back.

"Not yet," I begged him. "I know we're coming up on
something. Listen, the ocean isn't far away."

We stopped to listen. There was the sound of surf on
rocks and the high, bleating shrieks of seagulls going after
bait.

"This way," I said, and set out more to the left than we'd
been going. Five minutes later we came out on the rocky
shore of the big gray-blue bay, really the mouth of the
Sachem River, that scooped away down the coast toward
Newport. The view was so tremendous that I stopped in
awe.

Maybe the ocean is something you never get really used
to. With a cornfield, you watch it grow and know pretty
well everything there is to it. But an ocean hides whole
worlds underneath, millions of things that live and swim
and die and are born, unseen by human eyes. It can also
hide danger.

"Look, some fishing boats," Elliot said. "I'm glad I'm
not out there. I'd feel like a sitting duck."

"The Nazis would never waste one of their precious
torpedoes on a fishing boat."

"Yes, they would. In Maine, fishing boats have been getting picked off. I heard about this one case where a German
sub came up out of the water right in front of a trawler,
and the Germans started firing machine guns at the crew.

Everybody got shot dead except one guy who jumped overboard and hid underwater. He was rescued later and told what happened."

We gazed across the water, silent for a moment.

"Mike Parini says he saw German commandos come ashore on Briggs Beach a couple of nights ago," I said. "He reported it to the Coast Guard."

"How could he tell they were commandos?"

"He said they were wearing German military uniforms."

"German commandos would be stupid enough to wear their uniforms to invade America?" Elliot asked.

"No, Mike Parini is stupid enough to believe they would," I said.

We had a good laugh over this, then climbed down the embankment to the beach and set off along it. A stiff southwest wind had sprung up. It made the waves sit up and break into little white caps across the bay. Half a mile down, a high, wire mesh fence rose in our path. A sign posted on it read: "Entry Strictly Forbidden, U. S. Military Zone, Keep Out."

We came to a halt. The fence went out into the water too far to get around without swimming. The other end ran up the embankment and across an open field. We couldn't go that way without being seen. We were about to turn around when Elliot saw a strange pile of dead brush halfway up the embankment. I never would have noticed it but he'd see things like that. Whatever was different or out of place, Elliot's eye would catch it.

He was right about this brush. Underneath, we found a long slit that had been cut in the fence. Someone had been going in and out. We checked around to see if anyone was watching, then went through ourselves, pulling the brush over it again. We kept walking, staying close to the embankment so we couldn't be seen from above. After a while I told Elliot to wait a minute. I wanted to check where we were.

I climbed up the sandy bank. It was about twice the size of the one we'd come down and not easy to get toeholds in. When I got to the top, I raised up slowly on my knees, looked around, then dropped on my stomach and waved for Elliot to come. Fast.

"What is it?" he asked, when he came up, panting.

"You won't believe it."

We raised our heads together.

Across a short field, so close you could see the spring yellows and reds of the wild flowers growing in front, the gray barrel of one of the big guns stuck out from a huge concrete bunker. It was pointed straight over us. Elliot dropped his head fast.

"Bull's-eye!" I whispered.

"What if it fires?" Elliot asked, face down.

"The shell would go out to sea. It couldn't hit us. In fact, we're even too close to see anything. Let's go farther down the beach. We'll get a better angle."

Elliot thought this was one of the best ideas I'd ever

had. We slid back down the embankment and, keeping under its shadow, crept a few hundred yards farther along. Then I crawled up again and looked over.

"Perfect!" I mouthed back to Elliot.

When Elliot's head came up over the embankment this time, he saw we were a good distance beyond the big gun, and relaxed. We were now in a position to see all around the bunker and beyond to the fort, which wasn't just made of concrete like you'd think. There were regular wood houses, sheds and outbuildings, even some army tents pitched together on one side. They spread like a small village around the foot of a grassy hill that bulged up suddenly out of the land.

Everyone in town knew about this hill. You could see it from the road. It was the fort's battery, an operations center for the big guns and their one-ton shells. Underneath was a vast network of concrete rooms and storage chambers connected by wide underground corridors. The rooms housed the electrical generators, the communication systems, air conditioning and plumbing pipes, ammunition magazines, everything the fort needed to keep in a state of readiness.

There were two other camouflage hills in Sachem's Head, where smaller guns watched over the sea in other directions. In fact, the whole place was loaded with artillery, but secretly, so the Germans would never find it. A spy plane wouldn't have a clue what was here, even if it flew right over.

"See that house?" Elliot pointed to an ordinary-looking

farmhouse on a bluff not far away. "It's really a lookout. There's a hidden ladder that goes up the inside of the chimney. The windows are painted to look like they have curtains, but there are gun mounts in them. The whole house is made of cement. My father told me. I wonder if he's here?"

"Let's get closer. Maybe we'll see him."

We began to crawl on our stomachs across the field. Fifty yards in, we came to a stone wall where we could sit and spy out without being seen. A lot of soldiers were running around. It looked like something was getting ready to happen. We were too far away to see what.

"If the lookout spots something, how will the guns know where to aim?" I asked. They were too big to be moved by hand, anyone could see that.

"Everything gets reported to the plotting room," Elliot said. "You can't see it because it's hidden underground. That's where they do the calculations to work out the range and direction for the guns, so they can target enemy subs and ships exactly. All the charts are there, and they have radio contact with lookout stations up and down the coast and— "

A deafening roar drowned him out. The meadow rattled around us like a box of marbles. We fell on the ground and buried our heads under our arms. I thought Elliot would be a basket case for sure, and wondered if I'd have to carry him home. But after a few seconds he got his voice working and asked, "Was that the big gun?"

I was kind of shaken up myself. I knew it wasn't the big

gun, though, because no smoke was coming out of the barrel. The firing had come from somewhere else.

"I think it was one of the eight inchers."

"What were they shooting at?"

We sat up and looked out to sea. The fishing boats we'd seen before had gone home for the day. Farther out, the ocean was empty.

"I bet it was just practice," I said. "I heard they shoot the eights off every once in a while to be sure they're working right. If the big guns ever shoot, you'll know it, don't worry."

"How will I know it?"

"At this range? Your eyeballs crack."

Elliot looked at me. For about three seconds, I think he believed it, then he figured things out.

"That's not true, is it?" he said. "It's not true at all."

"It's not?"

"No. Anyway, your eyeballs don't crack. Grandpa told me. What happens with a loud noise is your eardrums get sucked out."

I stopped smiling. "They do?"

"Yes. They get sucked out and explode. Then they snap back in like old stretched-out rubber bands. It's very painful."

"It is?"

Too late, I saw that I'd fallen for the same sucker trick. Elliot was watching me out of the corner of his eye.

"Ha, ha," I said. "I guess it would be painful if it really happened. But it won't because what really happens is your veins erupt and blood spurts out your nose and ears. Then your lungs collapse and your kidneys turn hard as rocks."

"Is that so?" Elliot inquired coolly. "I guess that's why your skin begins to peel off and you turn purple all over?"

"Exactly."

"And then your whole body explodes."

"It's bad, bad. Luckily it's over so fast you never know what hit you."

"Or what didn't hit you," Elliot pointed out.

There was something warm and satisfying about this conversation that pleased us both. We looked out to sea some more in case anything interesting had come up, such as a shot-up German sub. Nothing had, so we crawled back through the field to the beach and started for home.

Far off, the church bell was ringing from the town commons. Six chimes. Six o'clock! We began to run to be in time for supper. The sun was in our eyes. I would never have seen the far-off figure coming toward us, but Elliot caught a flash of blue against the sand.

"Look!"

I shaded my face and saw him, too. Abel Hoffman. He was walking slowly up the beach, his stick keeping time as usual. His big canvas knapsack was on his back with the stool sticking out behind.

"He's been painting somewhere," Elliot said.

We waited for a minute, expecting him to turn off toward the road the way we had come, but Abel didn't turn. When he got to the wire fence with the army's sign to keep out, he climbed up the embankment, moved the dead brush aside, slipped through the slit in the wire and kept coming.

"Holy smoke, he knew it was there!" Elliot said. "He must have been here before."

"Maybe he made it," I said.

He was heading straight for us, now. Elliot looked around.

"Come on. I don't want to meet him."

We climbed up the sand bank again and lay flat behind some thorny beach plum.

Abel came heavily along, unaware that he was being watched. He passed below our hiding place and went on down the beach.

"Where's he going?" I whispered.

"To paint, of course," Elliot whispered back. "He must have a place he likes along this beach. I hope he doesn't get caught."

"A strange place to want to paint with a bunch of guns at your back."

"No, it's nice here. There's a beautiful view of the ocean and the coast up to Newport. I'd want to come here, too, if I were him."

"Well, he'd probably invite you if you'd just go see him."

Elliot turned his back and gazed across the bay. I knew he was mad I'd said that.

When Abel went out of sight, we slid back down to the beach and set off again. For a long while, we didn't talk. Elliot was mulling over something in his mind. I knew it was useless to ask him what. Anyway, I was doing some thinking of my own.

When we came out on the West Main Road, I said: "You know, it really is strange that Abel Hoffman should want to sneak in and paint on the bay beach. There are so many other beaches around. The view down the coast is even better on the other side of the harbor."

Elliot said nothing. I wasn't even sure he'd heard me. We walked home silently, side by side.

5

THE GERMANS STRUCK again at the end of the week.

Uncle Jake told us when he came in the kitchen for lunch. It was Saturday. He'd been over at the fort all morning working on a problem in the underground air-conditioning system and was there when the terrible reports began to come in.

"A big passenger ship was hit. The S. S. *Cherokee*, coming from England to New York City. She took two torpedoes early this morning."

"Where?" we gasped. Grandma, who was in the kitchen too, rolled her hands up suddenly inside her apron and turned away to the window.

"Just up the coast off Cape Cod. German subs did it. She went down real fast; nothing anyone could do. So far, they're counting more than eighty lost, about half those on board."

"Eighty!" We were all shocked.

"The Coast Guard was out there pretty fast picking up

survivors. Not fast enough, though. A lot of servicemen, army officers, went down. The fort's in a scramble. Everybody's shaken up."

Grandma turned back around and said she'd go and tell Grandpa. He was out seeing patients in his office.

"I guess now he won't grouse any more about me pulling the curtains at night," she said, sounding almost snappish for her.

Coast houses had been under orders from the fort since April to black out their lighted windows after nightfall. This was so the German subs couldn't see our big convoy ships passing against the lights on land. For some reason, Grandpa Saunders thought it was a dumb idea and he refused to do it. Every night there'd be a kind of tussle going on with Grandma running around pulling the shades and curtains and Grandpa getting too warm and yelling and yanking them open again.

I looked over at Elliot. He was staring at his hand as if he might start gnawing on it any time. I didn't ask if he wanted to go down to the fort. I didn't feel like going myself.

We went up to his room and sat around until supper, not saying much. Elliot worked over some drawings he was doing of different kinds of planes. He wasn't using sheet paper anymore. It was getting too scarce and expensive with the war on. He'd gotten hold of a whole roll of butcher's wrap, the light brown paper they use to wrap up meat in the store. Whenever he needed something to draw on, he'd put his ruler down for a tearing edge and take a piece off the roll. Maybe because of this new, unlimited source of paper, he'd recently gone into series drawing. First he'd drawn German submarines attacking ships at sea, then different armored vehicles he'd seen around town, then soldiers from the fort. Most recently he'd started on war planes.

Planes were always flying over Sachem's Head on coast patrol from Quonset, the navy air base on the other side of Newport. Some days, formations of B-24s would practice dropping incendiary bombs in the bay. Other times, there'd be a group of fighter planes staging dogfights in the sky right over our heads. We could spend a couple of hours easy just lying on our backs in some field, watching.

One day, a plane crashed in a field in Eavesville, the next town over from Sachem's Head. Elliot and I hitched a ride to go and see the wreck. When we got back, Elliot drew some good pictures. That seemed to get him going on planes. He drew fighters, bombers, reconnaissance and sea planes, all different kinds. That night, when I looked over and saw him drawing a B-17 Flying Fortress, I said:

"That's what my father's flying out of England. They're the biggest and go higher than the other bombers. My dad has to wear an oxygen mask or he can't breathe, and his flight suit is heated. It can go to sixty below up there."

"Aren't you scared he'll get shot down?" Elliot asked.

"No," I said, though I was sometimes if I stopped and thought about it.

I told Elliot about the dream I kept having, the one where a silver plane comes toward me in the air, and I see the shape of the pilot at the controls but can't ever see his face.

Elliot was interested. "Do you think it's your dad trying to get through to you?" he asked.

"Maybe," I said, though I didn't really believe it. I never put much faith in mystical stuff like that. "The thing is, I'm not even sure it's him. I try and try to recognize him but the pilot never turns his head. Then, I wake up without knowing for sure."

"Next time call to him," Elliot advised. "Maybe he's waiting to hear back from you before he shows himself."

"I wrote him three letters before we came here and he never answered them."

"Well, this is different. Call out. Tell him you've got to see him."

I said I'd do it if I could remember. Dreams don't always let you do what you want.

The delicious smell of Grandma's cornbread rolls drifted up to us. Just before we went downstairs for supper, a thought came into my mind.

"Do you think Abel Hoffman could have anything to do with the ships that are getting torpedoed off here?" I asked.

"How could he?" Elliot said. "Those hits were miles away."

"I don't know. Maybe he hears things and sends messages. He could have a secret radio transmitter. He has binoculars. I saw them around his neck when he went past on the beach. Maybe he watches for ships."

Elliot frowned and shook his head. "You're only thinking that because he's German. If it had been anybody else we saw down there, you never would have thought anything."

I had to agree that this was probably true.

The sinking of the S. S. *Cherokee* upset everyone even more than they'd been before. It was another step toward realizing that the war might be coming to our side of the ocean, and faster than we thought. Even Grandpa got worried. Up to then, he'd been against the forts and the guns, against everything that had to do with the army being in Sachem's Head. He thought having artillery on the point was ridiculous, a waste of taxpayers' money, and he looked down on Uncle Jake for working over there. The night of the *Cherokee*'s sinking, he was quiet about all that.

"U. S. Army officers on board, coming home, I hear. Went down with the crew, some of them," he said out of the blue.

The rest of us jumped on the subject. We talked about the rescue efforts, and what the fort was doing to beef up surveillance. Uncle Jake knew the details but with Grandpa staring down his gullet, he was too nervous to tell us very much. Grandma brought up her point about the black-out curtains again, which made Grandpa glare at her. You could see his heart wasn't in it though. After a pause, my mother asked:

"What were our officers doing coming back on that boat? They're supposed to be going over to fight, not coming back, aren't they?"

She looked and sounded tired out. She and Aunt Nan got a half day off from the torpedo station on Saturdays, but they'd spent that afternoon digging in Grandma's vegetable garden. They wanted to set up for a strong harvest in the fall. There were going to be more food shortages, they said. We'd already been on meat ration books for two months and were getting used to a lot more bread and potatoes. That night, besides Grandma's rolls, the main thing on the menu was leek and ham bone soup—not anybody's favorite but, in the spirit of patriotism, no one complained. Even Carolyn had figured out that the way things were, complainers occupied a category hardly better than traitors.

"They were officers being sent back to train new recruits," Grandpa said, in answer to my mother's question. "They'd had a taste of the fight so they'd know a thing or two."

I looked at my mother and I knew what she wanted to ask next. She was thinking about my dad, curious to know if army airmen were among those being sent back. Not that my father would have been among the victims on the S. S.

Cherokee. If he had been, she would already have heard. My mother wanted to know if it was possible that an American pilot might be reassigned back home to teach, if there was any chance my father might come back, away from the danger of his bombing raids over France.

My mother wouldn't ask this, though. She knew the rules. Nothing about my dad was ever mentioned in that house. Grandma might talk in a general way about "a bomb raid over France the newspaper reported yesterday." I might even catch her reading one of my mother's letters from Dad. But not with Grandpa around. He'd have to be out of the house, back in his office, before she or Aunt Nan could show any interest.

That night at supper, my mother kept respectfully silent again. Suddenly, it made me so mad I just went ahead and asked what she wanted to know for her.

"Were there any American pilots on that boat?" I said to Grandpa. "My father's an officer over there and he'd be a good one to send back to teach people. He used to be a test pilot and knows everything about B-17s."

The room went completely silent. Everyone stopped eating and looked at Grandpa. Elliot's mouth dropped open a little, as if he might be having trouble breathing.

Grandpa had set his water glass down just before I'd asked my qestion. When I finished, he snatched it up and got to his feet. His arm drew back and he looked ready to throw the glass down the table at me when his hand stopped and froze in mid-air. Rocking back on his heels, he roared out in a terrible voice:

"THERE WERE NO DAMN FOOL PILOTS ON THAT BOAT, OFFICER OR OTHERWISE! "

He shoved his chair aside and walked out of the room, the water glass still clenched in his hand. The way he was holding it, kind of high up and away from himself, it might have been a bomb with a hair trigger set to go off.

For a second after he left, everyone sat paralyzed. Then the spell broke, and Grandma cried out in a disapproving voice:

"Oh, Harvey! Language, language! Children are present!"

Just as she would have swept up the pieces of the water glass if he had thrown it, or wiped up a spill of gravy, she began the job of bringing the table back to order.

Carolyn was sent for more warm rolls in the kitchen. The water pitcher went around again, whether anyone wanted it or not. Talk started in fits. The new garden was brought up and summer squash came in for close examination.

"Now, crook neck," Grandma said. "I'm not sure what to do about crook neck squash. It won't can. Say what you will, it's not a canning vegetable."

"But it makes good pudding," Aunt Nan said. "We could do up a good batch of crook neck pudding. Also, there's crook neck soup."

"What do you think, Helen?" Grandma said, turning to my mother. "Shall we plant crook neck squash this summer, or try something with more cannability?"

"Oh, plant it, surely," my mother answered.

Something about her voice caught my ear. I looked up and saw two nearly invisible tears drop down the side of her face. She raised her napkin and smoothed them off with an impatient flick before even Grandma could see.

"I like crook neck squash!" Carolyn said. She was sitting next to my mother.

"We all love crook neck, don't we?" my mother said. She gave me a little smile, as if this were a family joke between the three of us. Then she reached out and put her hand protectively over the top of Carolyn's head, and said, "There's no need to can it or even make it into soup. Let's just plant it to have fresh whenever it comes up."

Whatever it was that needed fixing, that did it. Everyone started nodding and taking up their forks. Elliot's eyes stopped blinking crazily around. He really worried me sometimes, the way he looked. Aunt Nan went on a search for Uncle Jake's napkin under the table. Five minutes later, Grandma slipped away in the direction of the front parlor. She came back followed by Grandpa, who sat down and pulled up his chair as if he hadn't done a thing but go to take a telephone call in the hall.

That made me mad. It made me furious. I didn't say anything, though. Everybody else was so determined to pretend that nothing had happened. Somehow they'd all decided, without even talking to each other, to forget the whole thing. A scared feeling came into me when I saw that.

I had the idea there might be something really bad going on that I didn't know about.

After supper, Elliot went straight to his room while I stayed behind to help with the dishes. When I went up later to find him, he was sitting at his table, working on a drawing.

"Did you get it?" I asked.

He knew what I meant, but he just shrugged. He looked pretty worn out.

I came over and took a peek, and the picture was great. It was fantastic! It showed the whole dining room, everyone and everything just as it had been.

At the end of the table was Grandpa with the water glass raised and his mouth open in a shout.

"There were no damn fool pilots on that boat, officer or otherwise," Elliot had written in block letters underneath. Everyone was cringing in their seats. I saw myself cringing, too.

"Did I really look that scared?"

"Yes, you did."

"I thought he was going to throw the glass at me."

"I thought so, too, and so did Grandma. He's thrown things before."

"He has?"

"He threw the fire tongs at my father one time and hit him in the arm."

"The fire tongs! Why?"

"He doesn't like my father."

"But why?"

Elliot bit the end his pencil. He hated talking about personal things. Whatever he thought of his family, he kept it to himself. Mostly, I wouldn't even ask him.

"It's all right. You don't have to tell."

"Oh well," Elliot said, "I guess I can talk about it if I want. My father had a plumbing business. But he took a loan out from the bank and couldn't pay it back, so they took the business away, and also our house. That's why we had to move in here."

"Where was your house?"

"It's yours."

"You used to live in our cottage?"

"We used to own it. Until two years ago. Now the bank owns it. That's why it was up for rent."

Elliot tapped his pencil on the drawing. "We would have lost the truck, too, but Grandpa paid to buy it back."

"Then why did he throw the fire tongs?"

"He gets mad when he thinks people aren't doing the right thing. He threw a loaf of bread at my mother because she took the job at the torpedo station. He said it's not a woman's job, but she only did it to make money so we could move someplace else."

"Don't you hate him?" I asked. "I hate him. I know he's the reason no one can talk about my dad around here. I think they had a fight way back when he was young."

Elliot glanced up at me. For a moment, I thought he was

going to tell me something, then he looked down at his drawing.

"Grandma was afraid," he said. "She thought he was going to throw the glass at you. She knows he would do it if you made him mad enough."

I looked at Grandma in the picture. Her hand was over her mouth. It seemed to me she was getting ready to say, "Harvey! Language, language! Children are present!"—a silly thing to even bring up considering what was going on. Carolyn was the only real child there. You could just barely see her eyes over the table. She was trying to hide. She probably didn't even hear Grandpa swear. She was staring at the water glass in his hand, frightened to death.

I looked at my mother in the picture next, and I could hardly believe it. Elliot had seen my mom's tears. He'd seen them before I had, because he'd drawn them just coming up in her eyes, not big enough yet to roll out onto her face.

"Elliot, you are amazing."

"It's not finished yet."

He drew in some other details that must have been there but only he had seen. He put Aunt Nan's wedding ring on her knotted-up hand and drew Carolyn's bunny barrette in her hair. He made a greasy drip of soup on Grandma's big soup tureen and, leaning way over—by now his pencil was down to a stub—he shaded water into the glass Grandpa had in his hand. The glass was half-full.

"Was the glass that way?"

"Yes."

"How can you remember?"

"I just can."

Only one thing was ever left out of Elliot's drawings—Elliot himself. For some reason, I'd never thought of this before. Now it struck me, maybe because this picture seemed unfinished without him. After all, everyone else was there.

"Why don't you ever put yourself in?" I asked when he put the pencil down. "You never do, not in any of your drawings."

"Because I'm not in them," Elliot said. "I'm looking at them."

"But you're in them, too. You were sitting right here." I pointed to a spot off the drawing where his chair would have been if he'd left room for it on the paper.

"That would be true if I wasn't drawing it," Elliot said. "When you're drawing something, you can't see yourself because you're the one who's doing it. You're just drawing whatever's around you."

"Couldn't you imagine what you look like and put yourself in? Everyone knows what they look like, more or less."

Elliot frowned.

"I know what I look like, I just don't want to be in it," he said, sounding angry. I knew I'd better drop the subject.

Some other drawings were lying on the table. I walked around to have a look at them.

"What are these?"

"They're of the fort, from when we sneaked in."

He stood up and spread them out. There must have been eight or ten of them. I saw the big gun as we'd first seen it that afternoon, aiming over our heads out to sea.

"This is good. You got it perfect."

The cement farmhouse was there with its fake windows. There were the soldiers running back and forth in front of the man-made hill. He'd made a sketch of the big gun in profile, too. You could see the gray barrel sticking out from the bunker.

One drawing was not of the fort, but I couldn't figure out what it was. It was of a flat, field-like place with a lot of wavy lines and swirls running through it.

"What's this?"

Elliot gave a kind of embarrassed laugh.

"It's the ocean," he said, "but it didn't come out too well."

Before I could say anything else, he gathered up all the drawings and stuffed them away in the box under his bed.

6

ON JUNE 15TH, ten days after the sinking of the *Cherokee*, enemy torpedoes hit an eight-thousand-ton British freighter sixty miles east of Provincetown.

All that day, whenever we had a minute, Elliot and I listened to reports about rescue operations on the radio. We heard how everyone got off the ship in time, but then, since the boat was so slow to go down, the captain and first mate went back on board to save some equipment. In those few minutes, the ship suddenly rolled and sank, and they were lost. Worse, the German subs that did the damage—at least two it was thought—got away clean. It made you mad to think how those subs were probably lying out somewhere on the shallow sandy bottom off Cape Cod, waiting for the next ship to come their way.

It made you nervous, too. Elliot and I weren't the only ones listening to the radio. By evening, there probably wasn't anyone in town who hadn't looked to sea and worried what might be out there. That night, it was hard to go to sleep because planes kept roaring past overhead. Mom and I sat up for a while and watched the searchlights in Newport pan the sky for enemy planes.

About 3 A.M., after we were asleep, the air-raid siren at the end of our lane went off. We all jumped a mile in our beds. Carolyn began to cry, and we were getting ready to run up to Grandma's root cellar to take cover when the all-clear siren sounded. A wire malfunction had set the siren off, we found out the next day. That didn't stop us thinking about it the next night, though, or the night after that. You get the willies when you wake up to an alarm like that, even after you know it wasn't anything. Carolyn had to sleep in Mom's bed for a week before she got over it.

Grandpa must have gotten a jolt from that siren, too, because he began to talk to Grandma and Aunt Nan about making a bomb shelter. He'd refused to have anything to do with bomb shelters up to then, so this was a big turn-around.

Grandma said the cellar under the house was the best place for it, and told Elliot and me to sweep the whole place out, which just about broke our backs because it was so full of ancient dust and spider webs. We put blankets and pillows down there, canned food and some crocks of water.

"Now that we've got this blasted shelter, you can bet we'll never need it," Grandpa said. He was as glad to have it as we were though, and he began to be in favor of other security measures around our two houses.

At night, we all followed the fort's orders to curtain and even double curtain our windows, and everyone went to sleep with shoes and clothes laid out in case we had to evacuate fast. The fort had suggested that, too.

We carried sandbags and chicken wire up into the attic side of Elliot's room (our cottage didn't have an attic), and lumped it in a way to deflect fire bombs in case any fell through the roof.

"What about me?" Elliot said. "I won't deflect bombs. Shouldn't I sleep somewhere else?"

"You?" Grandpa said. "You have legs, I suppose. You can run downstairs."

Because he was often out in the evenings on house calls, Grandpa painted the top half of his car headlights black to keep them from shining up into the air. All car owners in Sachem's Head had been told to do this so enemy aircraft couldn't identify our roads or places of assembly after dark. Some people said it was a long shot that German war planes could make it across the ocean to bomb us, but the fort didn't want us taking any chances.

The town practiced for air raids, too. When the sirens went off in a certain way, we were supposed to run inside and take cover. After the first few alerts, Elliot and I didn't bother to do that anymore, but we were impressed when Grandma volunteered for Civil Air Patrol duty. Twice a week she went up the watch tower on Eavesville Road and spent an afternoon watching through binoculars for the approach of enemy aircraft.

"I saw three seagulls today," she'd tell us with a twinkly eye when she came back. Or, "An enemy plane approached and I notified headquarters. But it turned out to be that mothy old buzzard that lives down at the marsh."

Grandpa would frown when she made light of things like this, and stomp back to his office. He'd gone completely in the other direction by this time and become more serious about civil defense than any of us. From some closet in the house, he'd dug out an old star-gazer telescope that he kept trained on the bit of ocean he could see from his surgery window. He was as jumpy as anyone about spotting periscopes out there, and once called the fort to report an enemy sub that turned out to be Jimmy Potter raking clams in a rowboat off the point.

Not all sightings were groundless, though. We were well along in June when the newspapers reported the real thing—four Nazi commandos posing as fishermen had sneaked ashore at night on Long Island. They'd brought crates of explosives which they buried in the sand. Their plot was to come back and get them, and start blowing up our railway lines. They went to New York and Washington, D.C. first though, and were arrested before they could do anything. Still, the idea that they'd landed at all and got away with it, came as a big shock to everybody.

"How were they caught, did anyone say?" I asked Uncle Jake the morning after their capture had come out. He was eating breakfast at Grandma's, where I'd gone to pick up Elliot for our walk to school. Elliot was taking forever as usual, probably cataloging his birds' eggs or something.

"The Coast Guard was tipped off," Uncle Jake said, putting a spoonful of grape jelly in the center of his toast and smoothing it down.

"By who?"

"Somebody saw suspicious activity on the beach. A fisherman, someone said. But the Feds were onto them so quick, I think it could have been a code interception."

"You mean we intercepted a Nazi radio message?"

"Well, I don't know that officially, so don't go talking it around."

"Is that the kind of stuff they do at the fort?"

Uncle Jake cleared his throat and glanced over his shoulder. Seeing that Grandpa was nowhere in sight, he said:

"There've been other reports about German agents trying to land, up in Maine, down in the Florida Keys. The whole coast is on the alert. Fort Brooks is active, I'd say. One of the most active, the reason being we're in a particularly vulnerable position here in Sachem's Head."

"We are?" I loved hearing this kind of thing.

"Well look at us." Uncle Jake took a sip of coffee. "We're the most prominent point of land on the southeast coast, so close to the naval base in Newport we can almost touch it. Look at a map sometime, then think if you were the Nazi military command setting up for an invasion. Or not even an invasion yet—that would come later. Setting up for a secret agent or two to get ashore and pick up information. On our defenses, say, what kind of guns we have, where we have them. On the convoy ships, when they sail, where they'll pass so a U-boat can be waiting. Sachem's Head beaches would be the place to hunker down, it seems to me. It'd be the perfect place to set up a signal operation. You wouldn't even need a radio. A high-powered flashlight would do it, and a knowledge of Morse or some secret code."

A heavy clump of footsteps told us that Grandpa Saunders was arriving for breakfast. Uncle Jake grabbed his coffee cup and stood up.

"Gotta run," he said. "There's a stoppage over on Cold Pond Road." He picked up his plate and bolted into the kitchen.

Elliot still hadn't shown up. I knew he wouldn't come into the dining room while Grandpa was there. I got my books together and headed for the front door, thinking I'd wait in the yard. Grandpa spotted me before I made it.

"I see that boy's holding you up again," he called out. I had to turn around and face him in the hall or it would have looked bad.

"I guess so."

"I'd think you'd get tired of waiting for him after awhile."

"I don't mind."

Grandpa stared at me. "Well, I've got to hand it to you, you've been keeping him on the path of order and reason lately, something nobody else around here seems able to do."

"I try," I said, really feeble-sounding. It wasn't true either. No one kept Elliot on any path he didn't want to be on. I hoped he wasn't listening.

Grandpa came a couple of steps nearer and looked at me through his spectacles, eyes like ice picks.

"Ever thought of joining the medical profession?" he asked.

That kind of stopped me. I couldn't say anything.

"It's well-respected work, gets a steady income. Young fellow like you could do worse."

"I guess I haven't thought of it yet," I said. "I mean, I haven't thought of any profession yet."

"Well you'd best start! You come on back to my office some day, have a look around."

"Yes sir. Thank you."

"Are you planning a college education for yourself? Or are you going to be one of those that runs off looking for hare-brained adventure and wastes his opportunities?"

"Oh, college, yes, definitely."

"Well, good. That's settled. You come back to my office. I'll show you the ropes."

It was the last thing in the world I'd ever do. You couldn't have dragged me into that office. Luckily, Grandpa was done with me, though. He turned and went on into the dining room. I flung open the front door and was just going through when Elliot appeared behind me, carrying his coat and books. We charged out together.

"Where were you? I waited and waited!" I exploded when we got clear of the house.

"I was there," Elliot said, "waiting for you."

"No you weren't. Elliot, don't lie."

"Yes, I was. I was waiting in the back hall for you to stop talking to Grandpa."

"I wasn't talking. He was."

"He was giving you the big sell," Elliot said. "He wants everybody to be a doctor. Watch out. When he starts on that it means trouble. You better go see his office or he'll be yelling and insulting you next."

"He can yell all he wants, he can't scare me."

"That's what I mean," Elliot said, shaking his head. "Talk like that drives him crazy."

"He can't hear me."

"Be careful, that's all. He doesn't only yell."

"He throws the fire tongs, I know. Listen, have you seen Abel Hoffman around lately?"

"He's around." Elliot looked at me. "Why? Did Grandpa say something about him?"

"No. Your dad was telling me that Sachem's Head would be one of the best places for German agents to set up an operation. Because of our beaches, and being so close to Newport."

"So?"

"So all you'd need is a flashlight, he said. You could send messages out in code to the German subs."

"And binoculars?" Elliot said looking straight ahead.

"Yeah, I guess so."

"Some other people around here must have thought of that, too."

"What do you mean?"

"Abel Hoffman got beaten up last night."

I stopped walking. "How do you know?"

"He came by our house about midnight and knocked on the door. Grandpa took him out back to his office and fixed him up. They broke his arm."

"Who did?"

"Abel didn't know. Or wouldn't say. Some men jumped him in the road. He was coming back from somewhere and they were waiting in the woods near his place. It wasn't like a fight. They were out to get him. He looked pretty bad when I saw him. His face was all puffed up."

"How did you see?"

"I sneaked outside and watched through the window when they went into Grandpa's office. I heard them talking. No one else knows he was here and I'm betting Grandpa won't tell. He doesn't want to be associated with him. Don't you tell anyone either, okay? It might give other people ideas."

"You mean . . ."

"Right, to beat him up again, or worse."

"Would they do that?"

Elliot looked at me. "You're the one who said it: Sachem's Head is the perfect place for a German agent to set up operations. And who's the only German in town?"

"Abel Hoffman," I whispered.

7

SINCE THE MIDDLE of May, my mother had received no letters from my father. She didn't speak of it or show any sign of worry but, as the month of June wore on, I felt her need to hear from him growing more desperate.

She would wake at night and go around the house doing odd jobs, washing floors, ironing clothes, figuring house accounts. One night, she sewed a white banner with a blue service star on it to mount in our front window. Other families in town had these banners and I knew what they meant—that a person who normally lived in that house was in the war, gone to fight for our cause. You were supposed to be glad to have a star (some families had two or three) but the sight of my mother's gave me a sick feeling when she showed me and Carolyn the next morning.

"Dad doesn't live here, he's never lived here, so why does he need a star?"

"I think he'd be pleased to know we're supporting him wherever we are, don't you?" my mother said.

"But, do we really have to put it up? I think it's stupid. Everybody already knows who went to fight. Anyway, no one ever comes in this house except us. If no one can see it, why do we need one?"

"I thought you'd be proud to have one."

"I am, but . . ."

I wouldn't tell her the real reason. A few weeks before, a boy in our class at school, Willie Vogel, had heard by telegram that his father had been killed in action in the Pacific. It was the first war casualty in our town and we kids took sharp notice of it. For a couple of days afterwards, Elliot and I walked the long way to school, past Willie's house, to see what was happening there.

Aside from the curtains being drawn tight, probably against snoopers like us, there wasn't anything different. Nobody even looked like they were home. Then I noticed that the service star in the front window had changed color. It wasn't blue anymore, but gold.

"That means the person was killed," Elliot whispered.

"How do you know?"

"I heard someone say it. You change to gold so everyone will know that the person gave his life in the war. Because you'd feel too bad to go around telling people out loud, especially if it was your father."

This was too much for me. If my mother was superstitious about boasting about my dad, I was afraid of his blue star from the moment I saw it. Whenever I walked home to our cottage, I'd put off looking at the window where my mother hung it. I'd wait till the last second, when I couldn't help seeing it, scared stiff it had somehow changed. The thing was, that star made deadness seem too easy, a little matter of switching color while nobody was watching. It seemed that, just by having it, my father was bound to be killed. A few times, when my mother wasn't home, I tried to get rid of the banner by knocking it behind the radiator or pushing it under the door mat, as if the wind had come through. She would always find it though, and put it up again. To her, it was something to hold onto.

Sometimes at night, after I'd gone to bed, I would hear her go into the back of her closet and take out the shoebox of my father's letters she kept hidden there. It was on a shelf behind her hung-up skirts and blouses. The clothes hangers made a scraping sound when she pushed them aside. I would hear her sit on her bed (the walls were so thin in that cottage) and take my father's letters out of the box. The air-mail paper crackled, then there was silence and I knew she was reading.

I knew what she was reading, too, because I'd been in there myself, secretly, to find out what my father had to say about the war. Not the edited versions Mom read out loud to me and Carolyn at bedtime. Not:

"Today I arrived at our new air base and had the first really good meal since leaving the U. S. three months ago: steak and potatoes and did they taste fine!"

Not: "There are a lot of good fellows here. Tell Robert we play cards every night."

But: "Helen, last week I flew in the largest aerial assault on the enemy ever mounted by the RAF, over two hundred bombers. By now you'll have read about the big German-run tank factory outside Paris that was destroyed. Our rear gunner was shot going in but the rest of the crew came through. Others didn't fare so well, many good men went down. Best not to think too long on that score."

Also: "Dear Helen, I miss you tonight and am thinking of the farm. Thank God you three are safe back there. Our base was fire bombed by enemy planes. I am all right but our barracks was gutted and I lost much of my gear. This nothing compared to XXXXXXXXX"—the censor had marked out the town's name—"nearby which was most horribly attacked. The cathedral I visited only two weeks ago is now a smoking ruin."

For an hour or more I would hear the airmail paper crackle. Then, on some nights, came the small, watery sounds that told me my mother had begun to cry.

This I couldn't stand. I'd never seen her cry, not at the farm or here except for the two little tears she'd brushed away at the table. I thought she had no right to cry by herself like that, alone in her room where no one could help her. It wasn't fair, with my dad so far away. I would pull the pillow hard around my head and shut my eyes. I'd think about flying over Germany, dropping big ones, flak going off all around, or I'd be at the front line, mowing down Jerries with a machine gun.

The next day, walking with Elliot to school, I'd boast about my dad worse than ever, saying how he was actually in the barracks when it blew up, and saved somebody from burning to death, things that weren't complete lies, they might have been true, but they weren't exactly in the letters.

Elliot and I always walked to school in the mornings, but often in the afternoons we'd have different things to do, so we wouldn't wait around if the other person didn't turn up to walk home. As summer vacation approached, Elliot stopped appearing at all. One afternoon, though, he was waiting for me.

"Do you need to go home right now? There's something I want to show you," he said, and I knew right away from his voice that something was up.

"What is it?"

"A place I've been going."

"Where? You never told me."

"I am now."

He led me off the road to a path I hadn't noticed before. It headed into a forested area that people in Sachem's Head called "the back woods."

"You've been coming here? Nothing's here but a lot of swamp maples and mosquitoes."

"Abel Hoffman is here," Elliot said, with a careful

glance at me. "I've been visiting him in the afternoons. I thought you'd like to see where he lives. It's in a boat he's fixed up, a boat in the woods."

"You've been visiting him!"

"Don't be mad. I wanted to go by myself first, to see what it was like."

"You are the biggest liar."

"I know," Elliot admitted, "but I have to be."

He'd told me he was being kept after school by a teacher who was unsatisfied with his work. It had sounded true. His teachers were unsatisfied with him most of the time. To them, he was a goof-off with no ambition to improve. As far as I could see, they were right. He had his own interests, things so different from anything the teachers were trying to teach that he wasn't ever going to get along with any of them. Elliot needed another kind of teacher.

"Has Abel Hoffman been letting you use his paints?" I asked, as we walked along. You had to watch where you put your feet, it was that dense.

"Yes, he has."

"Have you been going to the bay beach?"

"No."

"So he's not painting the ocean anymore?"

"Yes, he is, but he doesn't go there anymore. Since he got attacked."

"Did he say who did it yet?"

"He knows, but he won't tell. He won't go to the police,

either. He doesn't trust them. Where he came from in Germany, the police were dangerous. If they didn't like you, they could have you arrested. They'd break down people's doors when they weren't home, smash their furniture, steal things."

"Did they smash up his house there?"

"His apartment. A couple of times."

We followed the forest path until it crossed a fast-running brook, then we veered off and walked beside the stream. The water made a loud chatter as it ran beside us over rocks and fallen trees. Elliot had to lean over and shout in my ear.

"Abel's still kind of beat up, but pretend you don't notice, okay? He doesn't want to talk about it."

We came to a small field, well shielded on all sides by trees and undergrowth. At the far end was something that looked like an overgrown haystack. When we walked nearer I saw it was a boat, a big old round-bottom sailboat that somehow must have been dragged up through the fields from the shore.

It was set in a low ship's cradle and rode as upright on the field as it must have at sea. But around and over the cockpit, a small house had been built with pine plank walls and a broad thatched roof, glass-paned windows and a door that opened and shut on real hinges. Out of this door, Abel Hoffman came in his blue cap.

"Cheerio! Cheerio! With great pleasure I am to see you!"

He rushed toward us, waving his good arm. The other lay in a sling against his chest, set in the plaster cast Grandpa must have made for him. More than a week had passed since the attack, but Abel's face was still in bad shape. His eyelids were dark and puffy, his lips were cut, a purple and yellow bruise ran all the way down one side of his head to his neck. He was limping, too.

The broken arm was his right, a lucky thing, Elliot had told me, because he was left-handed and his work hadn't been interrupted. He couldn't shake hands though. Instead he politely touched my shoulder, and gave Elliot's a friendly pat.

"So! You have bringing your cousin! At last! Vel-come! Please, I show you."

He walked me around his encampment, very proud. You could tell he'd been there for awhile. There was a good-size stack of chopped wood by the house, a vegetable garden fenced off with wire mesh, a water hole dug in the side of the brook that ran through the woods behind, paths leading in different directions. A beautiful red-tailed hawk was sitting on a tree limb near the boat. When we went by, it didn't move, just stared straight at us as if it owned the place. "My always friend," Abel said.

Far off, through leaves, I caught a glint of water.

"What's there?"

"It's the bay," Elliot answered. "We're closer than you'd think after coming through the woods."

Abel Hoffman began a scrambled explanation that completely lost me, so Elliot translated. He was a lot better at understanding Abel's English than I was. It made me wonder how long he really had been coming here.

"Abel says the bay is about a mile away. In winter, he has a better view. But it's an easy walk to the beach, and that's how the boat must have come to be here.

"The house was already built on. He thinks another artist had it before, because of carvings that were on some beams inside, and an old case of watercolors he found. The hull had rotted out in places, but he patched it and rebuilt the room inside. The roof is dried cattails. There's a wood stove inside that was already there. Do you want to look in? He says you can if you want."

"All right."

I walked up a short ladder and stepped into a tiny room where paintbrushes, rolls of paper, string, tacks, and other painting gear was stored neatly on shelves along the walls. Everything in the whole place was tucked, folded, hung, strung, stacked or shelved away. I saw a fishing rod, an ax and his binoculars, a cooking pot, a kerosene lantern, his thin wood walking stick. Behind some bedding tucked under a long bench, I saw a half-full bottle of whiskey.

The smell of turpentine and paint was thick but no painting was going on there at the moment. Abel had set up a sort of painting desk outside. When I stuck my head out the studio door again, I saw him standing in front of it with

Elliot, shouting and flinging his good arm around. It was an odd thing to see them together like that, one so passionate and excited about everything while the other stood quiet, looking almost bored. Only if you knew Elliot very well could you tell that he was taking in every word.

"Come! See! I am finish. I mean finish-ed!" Abel called when he saw me.

I came out and looked over Elliot's shoulder at his painting.

"What is it?" I asked. All I could see was a kind of swirl, blues and yellows, greens and pinks. And something dark under the colors, a shadow swimming deep below the surface.

"It's one of his ocean paintings," Elliot said. "Isn't it beautiful? It's of the bay."

"It is?"

"I paint the ocean! Out of my heart!" Abel shouted. "I see in the ocean. Many things. A storm coming . . . here," he pointed to his brain. "I paint!"

"A storm?"

Elliot jumped in to interpret.

"It's not the outer world but the inner world he paints. That's why you can't always recognize real things. He's painting his feelings."

I'd never heard of art like this before, and certainly never seen it.

"Nice," I told Abel. "Very good." Really I thought the painting was stupid. The poor guy couldn't even draw.

Everything looked messy, as if it had been flung on in a rush. If Abel's name and photo hadn't been in Elliot's book, I would have thought he was a fraud.

Abel's work table had some other things on it. I glanced down and saw a pile of drawings that looked familiar. They were Elliot's airplane series. He must have decided to bring them to show Abel after all. I recognized my father's Flying Fortress and a drawing of the crashed plane in Eavesville. Next to that were some of his drawings of the fort, the big guns, and Elliot's talent just shone out from them. They made Abel Hoffman's painting look like a little kid's.

But in the next hour, I watched how kind Abel was to Elliot. He let him use his brushes, his paper, any paint he wanted. I watched Elliot draw for him, and saw how happy Elliot was when Abel praised his lines. Elliot was drawing the boat-studio, the thatched roof, the tangled forest behind.

"This is good, so good," Abel told him. (He pronounced it "goot.") He took Elliot's pencil, added something to the drawing, and handed it back.

"I see. Like this?"

"Why not?"

"So, it doesn't need to be so . . ."

"Less perfectness," Abel Hoffman told him. "More . . ." He didn't know the word. "More you-ness," he said finally.

"You-ness?"

"Pardon . . . I mean, is coming from you, inside, who you are, here." He reached out and put his hand over Elliot's heart.

"Did you really like Abel's ocean painting, or were you just being nice?" I asked Elliot on the way home later.

"I liked it. I thought you did, too."

"Well, sort of. But it looks to me like he isn't a professional, yet. Maybe he has a way to go before he gets to that stage."

Elliot laughed. "Why would he be in a book if he wasn't a professional?"

"I don't know. Was that really him?"

"Yes it was. He was a teacher, remember? His paintings were in museums, until the Nazis came. They hate modern painters and don't want them around. He told me he was lucky to get out. Some didn't."

"What do they do, put them in prison?"

"I guess so. He won't say what happened. He doesn't like to remember, that's why he drinks."

"I saw his bottle. So he gets soused all the time?"

"Not all the time."

"Have you asked him why he's living here yet?"

"No! Come on, Robert, don't be so suspicious. He came here to work. What's wrong with that? He's going to let me paint with him all summer."

It was a bad idea, I knew it right away.

"Elliot . . ."

"Abel invited me," Elliot said. "He thinks I have talent."

"Well of course you have talent! But when people find out you're visiting him all the time . . ."

"They're not going to find out."

"Oh, sure."

"I'm being careful."

"It's not safe for Abel either, you know. He'll get it again."

"He's being careful, too."

"That's so stupid! This is a small place. Everyone finds out everything. Anyway, Abel is nowhere near as good as you are already. You can draw ten times better."

"No I can't." Elliot looked at me, shocked. "Abel's fifty times better. He doesn't want to draw like that, that's all. Drawing isn't anything. He says anyone can do it if they practice. It's not important. Abel knows what's important. He's going to show me stuff I would never get to know otherwise."

"Elliot, this is nuts."

"I wouldn't. Because who else would ever come here and show me? Nobody else," Elliot said. "Nobody else is ever coming here like him. He's the only one and this summer, he's going to teach me."

8

THE DRY SPELL in my father's mail lasted until the final
days of June. Then, like a bad joke, the mailman delivered
three letters at once to our old mailbox on the lane. My
mother had to sit down to recover after she came in the
house. Afterwards, she opened them one after another, and
read out parts to us, and we were all happier than we'd been
in weeks.

"Everything is all right! He sounds fine, doesn't he!" she
kept saying, as if she didn't quite believe it. You could see
how far down she'd been without news. Meanwhile, I noticed something about these letters. They had all been forwarded from the farm, not addressed to us in Sachem's
Head. I didn't bring it up right then. I waited until later,
after my sister was put to bed, and my mother was back
downstairs. Then I said:

"Dad still doesn't know we're here, does he?"

She was folding laundry and didn't look up.

"He wrote his last letter May 25th, and he still didn't

know," I said. "Does that mean he hasn't gotten any of our letters since we moved?"

"I guess it does," my mother said, avoiding my eyes.

"But that's four months!"

"Maybe he didn't get the letters that told him."

"Well write him again," I said. "He should know."

My mother nodded and we said no more.

I'd been wondering right along why my father was taking so long to hear about our move. After this, I began to suspect my mother of not telling him. I knew from the way she skipped around when she'd read from the new letters that she was keeping something back. Not just the usual blood and war stuff she thought we couldn't handle. Something else. Starting right then, I watched for a time when I could sneak into her closet and read the letters for myself. It didn't come up for a while, though. Life got busy all of a sudden.

After school let out for vacation, Grandpa was worried we'd get into trouble without a job, so Elliot and I were set up to work for Grandma around the house. We had to hoe and water the vegetable garden, prune the privet hedges, weed the driveway. We raked out the hen house, cut the grass, and every day we had some special job assigned to us that Grandpa thought up. This was light work for me compared to what I'd done at the farm, but to Elliot it was murder. He wasn't used to outdoor labor.

Too much sun gave him headaches. He got dizzy when

he had to stand up on a ladder to clip anything. If he pushed the grass mower for more than ten minutes, he'd start staggering around like a sick mule. I was the person who did most of the work. After a week or so of this, Grandma began to feel sorry for me, and even sorrier for Elliot who looked so miserable. She'd let us off early in the afternoons so we could go swimming.

Grandpa protested whenever he found out. He said Grandma wasn't doing us any favors by letting us skip out. Hard work was good for us. It built up a sense of responsibility. He said it was especially good for Elliot, who had no clear idea what hard work was. In fact, Elliot owed him a day's labor for all the food he ate, free of charge, and for the laundry that Grandma did for him, and the bed he slept in.

"Everybody does their part in this house, whether they like it or not," I heard Grandpa roar at him more than once. "I'm not in the business of housing freeloaders!"

Elliot must have felt insulted by all this, but he never showed it. He'd hang his head guiltily and even nod in agreement. The first chance he got, he'd scoot like a rabbit and get away.

"Don't run off like that. It makes you look bad," I said one time. He didn't get it, though. His idea was the less fight you put up, the better.

"I let the wind blow through," is how he said it to me once. "I let it blow and when it stops, I get up and go on."

"Well, at least you don't have to nod and agree all the

time while the wind is blowing!" I told him. "Don't you get mad?"

"It wouldn't help."

"I know, but don't you anyway?"

"The thing is, I have to live here."

I was glad I didn't have to live there. Much as I tried, I could not let Grandpa's wind blow through. Something always snapped and I'd end up fighting back, especially when Elliot was the target. To watch how Grandpa treated him made me furious.

"He worked all yesterday on the turnips!" I'd yell, even if it wasn't strictly true. Or, "No one can push that mower. It needs a grease job, that's what!"

Grandpa would swing his old nose in my direction and take me on at full blast. Then, if we were lucky, Grandma would rush in with her "Now, now, Harvey. You let the boys go about their business."

If we weren't lucky, I'd be left manning the fort alone, so to speak, because Elliot would slip away the minute Grandpa's eye was off him. It wasn't his fault. He just couldn't take the heat.

You had to be pretty tough to face the old man by yourself. By the end of our battles, I'd usually feel I'd held my ground with him, or if not, that at the least I was recognized. More than once, he asked again if I'd like to come back to visit his office. But I always got out of this somehow.

It was an afternoon after one of these stand-offs that

Grandma Saunders beckoned me down the hall to the spare bedroom and quietly closed the door behind us.

"You've been asking for a picture of your father," she said. "I have one here."

She opened the drawer of a tall bureau and took out a photograph in a silver frame. We sat down on the bed and looked at it together. A dark-haired, serious-faced boy in long pants and a hunting cap stood in a field with a shotgun in his hands. A spaniel sat by his feet, its tongue lolled out.

"He was about twelve, I think," Grandma said. "That's his dog, Baron. They'd go off together and come back with a duck or some grouse. He got us a thirty-pound turkey for Christmas one year. I'll never forget the size of that bird."

"He never told me he hunted. We didn't have a gun at the farm."

"Oh, he was a good shot," she said. "Your grandfather had him out hitting cans off a log before he was ten. He must have given it up when he went out to Ohio."

"You know, you can tell it's my dad," I said. "He looks like himself. Just younger, and his leg is right."

"What's right about it?"

"Well, you know, it's kind of bent a little now, from the plane crash. They never did get it put back together the way it was."

"I didn't know he was in a plane crash," Grandma said. "Was it after you were born?"

"Oh no. Way before. Before he met my mother, even. He was flying for the mail service. He said it was his first job, before he got the hang of things."

Grandma was quiet after this. We both looked at the photo some more.

"My father didn't keep very close contact with you, did he?" I asked finally.

"Never has," she said. "That's why I'm so glad you're here. You're like him, you know."

"I am?"

"You look like him a bit. And you've got his hard-working spirit. He was always a great help to me around this place, just like you are now."

I felt pretty happy hearing this, after Grandpa. "I bet you're just trying to make me feel good."

Grandma smiled and shook her head, then looked serious again.

"You remind me of him in another way. You've got your rights and you stand by them."

"I do?"

"Yes. Your father was the same. It came out stronger the older he got. He and your grandfather didn't get along too well over the issue of your father's rights. I thought you should know."

"I guess I've already figured out they didn't get along."

"Well, I'm glad," Grandma said, turning her head to look at me, "because sometimes I worry. Your Grandpa has a temper. It'd be better if you didn't stir him up if you could help it."

"You mean—"

"I mean don't let him pull you into fights, Robert. You step back, the way Elliot does."

"Elliot! He gives up everything," I said in disgust.

"Not everything," Grandma said. "He's a smart boy. You watch and see how he does it."

She stood up and shut the photograph of my father away in the bureau drawer.

Elliot was nowhere around when I came back from talking to Grandma. He'd gone to Abel's, I was pretty sure. I hated it when he sneaked off like that and left me behind. I went home and lay around and read a book for a while. Then I remembered the thing I'd been wanting to do.

The shoebox was there in its hiding place behind my mother's clothes. I carried it outside, down to a shady part of the backyard where it was cooler. When I opened the lid, my father's three new letters were sitting right on top, addressed to my mother, care of the farm, forwarded by the post office in Ohio.

For a minute I sat there, taking in the familiar look of his steeply slanting handwriting. It was strong, confident writing, and made me think of the hunting picture Grandma had showed me, of how strange it was that my dad never had a gun at the farm. He'd never breathed a word that he could shoot. He could have taught me, too, if he'd just said something. A lot of kids I knew had guns and went hunting with their dads. I would've loved to learn.

I picked up the first letter. It was dated in early May, written, like all the others, on a single page of thin airmail paper that folded up to make an envelope around itself. I opened the letter and read to the end without stopping.

Dear Helen,

We came through a tremendous battle this morning. German fighter planes ambushed us over the channel as we were heading home and shot down ten B-17s in our squadron.

They came out of nowhere and we were bone-tired besides after a night of heavy bombing. Many good men went down. It's hard on the base when it's like this. Flight patrol is still out looking for wreckage but so far no word. Roger White is among the lost, the flyer from Indianapolis. We came over together.

Our craft was damaged in the wing and the fusillage but worse our navigator was shot through the neck. We brought him home as fast as we could, but not fast enough. He died on the plane before we could get him off. I wish now I'd flown back low and taken the chance of some flak. He would have had more air. His oxygen mask was shot and not working right.

It's weighing on me if I did all I could. I can only say I flew like the dickens.

I am all right otherwise. We fly at night under cover of dark, and though it's hours of cold work we have good commu-

nication and know we are making our targets.

    I think constantly about you and the children, and the farm. Did the new wheat get in all right?

    Love, Kenny.

My mother had read Carolyn and me some of this letter already, leaving out the part about his friend going down, and the navigator. She'd also left out the mention he made of the farm and the wheat getting in, as if she hadn't wanted us to know he didn't know where we were. So, what was going on?

When I opened the second letter, I knew the problem wasn't my father not getting our mail.

Dear Helen,

Are you still at the farm? Your last two letters have been post-marked IL, it looks like, or is it RI? They're stamped all over. Probably the crazy war mail again.

The rest of the letter was familiar, except for one description of flying a bombing run that must have frightened my mother too much to share with us.

    Light flak is a pretty sight coming toward you—green, white, red—like a waterfall upside down. But if it hits you, there is a rending of metal and then a tinkling of glass, and it's time to get out of there. You don't know what it is to be really scared until you're up in the sky, your cover gone, and you see an ME-109 coming at you out of nowhere, guns blazing. My

gunners are the best, though, and we shoot back as good as we
get so you mustn't worry.

When I'd finished reading my father's letters, I returned them to the box exactly as I'd found them, and put the box back on the closet shelf. That night, I looked more closely at my mother than I had for a while, trying to think why she hadn't told my father about Sachem's Head. I couldn't stand not knowing the reason for it, and decided to ask her straight out. She was just coming down from reading Carolyn a bedtime story when I put it to her.

"Have you really written Dad about us being here?" I demanded. "You know, if he hadn't been getting our letters since January, I think he would've said something when he wrote back."

My question caught her off guard. She stopped at the bottom of the stairs and gazed at me. For a minute I thought she'd seen through me and guessed I'd been into her closet. Then she sighed.

"You're right. I haven't told him."

"But why? Are you afraid he'll be mad we left the farm?"

"Not that. Something else. I intended to tell him. As soon as we came, I intended to surprise him. But now . . . oh, it's so complicated." She came and sat down on the couch across from my chair.

"I do still mean to write him. It's just that every time I gather myself up to do it, I, well, the trouble is, I didn't realize how distant he was from his parents. He never talked much about them at the farm. They lived so far away. I could see they weren't a close family, but that's not so unusual, is it? I realize now that more happened between them than he let on."

"What happened? Did you find out?"

"That's part of the trouble. No one will say."

"Can't Aunt Nan tell you?"

"I think she knows but she won't talk about it. It's the same with Grandma and Uncle Jake."

"Elliot knows. They must have told him," I said. "But he'll never say anything about family stuff. It was something between Dad and Grandpa, I think."

"Long ago," my mother nodded. "A disagreement of some kind."

"And then Dad left and never came back."

"But it's so strange! Why did he never tell me? He never seemed angry at them. How was I to know? And now, here we are in the last place in the world he would wish us to be, I suppose."

"It's not your fault. Grandma invited you to come."

"Yes." My mother shrugged. "I don't understand it."

We sat without speaking while, outside, the sun sank slowly and shadow darkened the lawn. Daylight lasted until after nine o'clock during these long July days. Carolyn was nearly always asleep before sunset. As the room grew dimmer, my mother rose to pull the black-out shades so we could turn on the lamps.

"Do we have to have those down tonight? It's so hot, even with the windows open," I said. "Let's leave the lights off."

My mother nodded, and went back to the couch. We both sat quietly as various dusk noises swam in through the windows, chirps, croaks, the beat of wings overhead. Beneath these came the mournful horn of the channel buoy in the bay off Parson's Lane. "Old Bull" I'd heard it called around town and it was true that, when you stopped to listen, a bull was what it sounded like, a sad and lonely bull left behind in a field when the rest of the herd had gone home to the barn.

My mother must have been listening to it, too.

"It's not that bad here, is it?" she asked suddenly. "I mean, are you getting on all right?"

"It's okay," I said. "Don't worry about me. The person who needs worrying about is Elliot."

"Elliot?"

"Did you know that Elliot draws? He can draw anything, better than anyone I've even seen. It's the only thing he cares about."

I wished I could tell her about Abel Hoffman, but I couldn't. That would just get Elliot into trouble.

"Elliot draws?" my mother said. "I didn't know."

"Dad did. He sent him a book about modern artists last year, for his birthday."

"Yes, I remember. He was worried about Elliot. When he heard from Nan that they were going to move in with your grandparents, it worried him. I don't know why."

My mother sat up. "I almost forgot. We had a notice from the fort. They're going to fire off the big guns at ten o'clock tomorrow morning."

"Tomorrow! Why?"

"It's another military exercise. The concussion will be severe. We're to leave the windows open on either side of the house so the impact goes through without cracking the glass. And put breakable china away. I'll wrap things up tonight but tomorrow I'll be at work. Will you stay and keep an eye on the house?"

"Elliot and I are supposed to work on Grandma's hen houses tomorrow."

"I'll speak to her tonight and get you both off. You can take Carolyn up there in the morning and come on back."

"Do I have to?" I asked. "If we don't have to work, I want to be down closer to the fort to watch."

"Please, Robert? I'd feel so much better knowing some-one was here. Then you'll have the day off to do what you want."

I gave in and nodded. She went to tell Grandma while I sat on, watching the long beams of the searchlights play over Windmill Hill. I thought of my father, how he'd have to fly smart and fast to come through such lights to drop his bombs on the Germans; very smart and very fast to get past the guns waiting below to blast him out of the sky.

It wasn't very long after this that I realized I'd made a

mistake. Whatever I'd just promised my mother, I wasn't going to be here tomorrow, hanging around the cottage when the big guns went off. I couldn't be. I had to be there, with them, down on the bay beach, watching.

9

I DRAGGED CAROLYN out of bed early the next morning and took her up to Grandma's house.

Since school had let out, we'd been getting up whenever we wanted, eight or even nine o'clock, long after my mother left for work at seven. I'd cook some eggs or a little bacon for us, and wash up after. Cooking and taking care of Carolyn were things I'd learned how to do at the farm. There'd been times when both Mom and Dad had to get out early for spring planting, or to bring in a crop that was threatened by weather. Carolyn was used to me being in charge, but that morning she was mulish. She didn't like being woken up with no warning.

"Why do we got to go to Grandma's now?" she complained sleepily as we headed up the lane. "Anyway, I'm sick of being there all the time. There's nothing to do. Let's go to the beach."

"We can't today."

"Why not?"

"They're firing the big guns at the fort this morning. After I drop you off I've got to go back to the cottage and look after things."

"But, aren't you going to watch?" Carolyn asked me.

"Watch what?"

"The big guns."

"No, I'm not," I lied. "Mom told me to stay with the house."

"You aren't going to, though, are you," Carolyn said, after a look at my face. "I bet you're going to watch the guns."

"Why do you think that? I just said I was going home." I glanced down at her. She'd turned six that spring and begun to think she was smart.

"Well, I think you are because you got to," Carolyn said coolly.

"I don't know what you're talking about," I said, and walked her along faster. But a few minutes later, as we were coming up on Grandma's kitchen door, I thought I'd better cover my bases so I said:

"You wouldn't tell on me, would you?"

Carolyn shook her head. "I wouldn't."

"I'll do the same for you someday."

"Okay, and will you take me to the beach, too? I never get to go."

I promised I would when the right time came. We caught each other's eyes and kind of smiled because it was the first real bargain we'd ever done together.

My idea was that Elliot and I would go down to the bay beach together the way we had before, but:

"I can't. I've got plans," he told me when I went up to his room.

"I guess I know what they are," I said angrily.

"So what?" Elliot fired back. "I can do what I want."

He'd been spending more and more time with Abel Hoffman. It was beginning to get to me. Whenever I said anything though, he'd blow his stack and tell me I was against him like everybody else.

"I'm not against you. I'm worried about you."

"You're against Abel, too."

"I am not! I think it's terrible what happened when he got beat up."

I really wasn't against Abel in the beginning. I even went to visit him with Elliot a few times after that first time. I knew I shouldn't do it, but Abel was a sort of fascinating person, and the forest around there was old and full of Indian arrowheads. I could fish or wade in the rocky brook that ran nearby. Or I'd lie in the sun watching Abel's hawk dive on mice in the field. I'd never seen a bird hang around a person that way, though I'd heard about crows being picked up as babies and learning to depend on humans. Abel's hawk wasn't like that. He kept his distance and his own way of life, but he was attached somehow, I could see. He kept an eye on Abel, day and night. Once I asked Abel if he fed him to keep him around like that. He said no, it was all the hawk's idea.

Whatever I ended up doing at Abel's, Abel and Elliot would be doing their art. This was mostly a matter of standing around looking at Abel's paintings, I found out. The German had a big ego and liked to show off. Elliot would completely fall for this. He'd listen all afternoon without realizing that Abel hadn't said one word about him or his work. He only talked about himself and his crazy ocean paintings.

I noticed other things, too. Abel wasn't always such a polite and friendly guy. He had dark moods when he wouldn't talk or even look at us when we came. He'd just go on painting or cleaning brushes or stretching his canvases. If we got in his way, he'd be angry, and once he cursed at Elliot in German, and sort of spat at him.

"Don't worry about it," Elliot told me later. "He gets pent up when he's trying to do something that isn't working."

"So he spits at you?"

"He spits at whatever's near him. He hasn't had the easiest time, you know."

It was the excuse Elliot always brought up to defend Abel. I didn't agree with it, though I could see things were hard for the man. He was alone most of the time. His boat-studio was ingenious, but no substitute for a house. When it rained, the place got sodden and smelly. On hot days, it was like an oven. All kinds of bugs lived inside. Most of the time, Abel lived outside, eating sandwiches and fruit. He didn't like to cook. Fire smoke damaged his paintings, he said.

He was always worried about his paintings. He stored them in a shed he'd built a bit away from the boat. He was terrified they would get injured somehow—wet by rain, chewed by mice, mildewed in the salt air or dried out by the sun—and he'd thought up all kinds of ways to keep them safe.

He'd added layers to the shed roof, made gutters, built special racks for the big paintings so they wouldn't lean up against each other. The smaller paintings he wrapped in blankets or burlap, but then he'd get nervous and unwrap them to see if they were still okay. You didn't want to get too near him when he was in one of these unwrapping fits. He'd scream at you to get away. Just scream, like a lunatic.

"You know why he acts like that, because he's drunk," I said to Elliot one day.

Elliot shrugged. He knew. We'd both smelled the stuff on his breath.

"Well, you should watch out," I said. "Abel could forget who you are and hurt you."

"Watch out for yourself," Elliot shot back. "You're not my babysitter." After that, he went to Abel's without me. I didn't say anything. There were plenty of other things I could do with my time.

With all this, I guess I shouldn't have been so surprised that Elliot wouldn't come with me to watch the big guns. But I was surprised. And hurt. The firing of those guns was an event of special importance to me. I stormed downstairs, where Grandma finished me off by saying she had a meeting to attend at the church that morning. She couldn't take care of Carolyn till after lunch.

"Now you'll have to take me with you!" Carolyn said, as we plodded back down the lane to our cottage.

"Where?" I was in a frustrated rage by this time.

"To see the big guns fire. You have to take me, right?"

"You can't go there."

"Yes I can!" Carolyn shrieked. "You promised! I said I wouldn't tell and you promised you'd take me to the beach when the right time came."

I looked over at her.

"You promised," Carolyn said. "I could tell on you otherwise."

"Not if I don't go."

"But you've *got* to go!"

It was bad, I know, but I agreed to take her. No being scared, I said. She'd have to lie down when I told her. We got some wadding cotton off the roll in the bathroom cupboard for her ears and, after we'd opened the cottage windows, we set off.

By 9:30, we were already turning into the swampy thickets that grew between the road and the bay beach. We hadn't gone very far in when Carolyn's cheek got scratched by a thorn bush and began to bleed. We went back to the road.

"It doesn't hurt," Carolyn said. She was afraid I'd send her home.

We used her cotton to blot up the blood. The cut wasn't really so bad. She still had plenty of cotton left to stick in her ears. For fun, she stuck it in right then. A soldier riding by on a bicycle saw her do it and laughed.

"Getting ready for the big bam?" he called out. She nodded and he waved and rode on past.

We turned into the thickets again and, after a long thrash, came out on the bay. We slid down the bank to the beach the way Elliot and I had before, and walked fast to the military fence. The hidden slit was still there. We crawled through. I was sure Carolyn would start complaining about something, but she didn't. She followed behind me the whole way, quiet and serious.

I wanted to get to the stone wall in the field where Elliot and I had spied on the fort before, but far down the beach I saw a soldier patrolling with a rifle on his shoulder. Then I saw another soldier, much nearer, come out from the shadow of the embankment and stand still, looking away to sea.

Quick as I could, I pulled Carolyn in close to the embankment.

"They've put guards out. We'll have to climb up here."

"Where? There's no place."

It was so steep I had to half-haul and half-push her up. I was sure the soldier would hear us. Rocks and sand sputtered down onto the beach behind us. He never looked around, though. When we got up, we lay flat for a while just in case. Then I rose up slowly on my knees and took a peek into the field we'd climbed up to.

It was lucky I'd been careful. About a hundred yards away, somebody was standing with his back to us. His arms were folded across his chest and he was looking toward the fort, to where the cement bunkers for the big guns opened out of the artificial hill not more than a quarter mile off. In three seconds I knew who it was. Abel Hoffman.

I dropped back down beside Carolyn and kind of caught my breath.

"What is it?" she whispered.

"A man. Stay down."

After a while, I stuck my head up again. Abel hadn't moved. He was still staring the same way at the guns. Elliot wasn't going to find him at home if he went visiting this morning, that was for sure. I told Carolyn we could try sneaking forward a little into the long grass. We crawled on our bellies until we found a place where the view of the guns was better. We could see their gray barrels now, extended from the bunkers, aiming out to sea. I was so excited I got a chill up my spine.

I kept checking on Abel. He was looking at the guns through binoculars, now, arms held taut. His plaster cast was gone. He shifted his weight, made a quarter turn to the right, and stared through the binoculars out to sea. I pulled Carolyn down. She'd been standing up, trying to see better.

"Keep your head below the grass. Where's your cotton?"

"Right here. I couldn't hear anything so I took it out."

"Well put it in again."

"Are the guns going to shoot soon?"

I showed her my watch, then remembered she couldn't tell time. "It's two minutes of ten. Get ready."

From across the field we'd been hearing a low grinding or cranking noise. I began to realize it was coming from the guns. When I looked more closely, I saw that their barrels were being slowly raised. The cranking stopped, started again, stopped. Started. Finally, when the guns were pointed steeply up toward the sky, the grinding stopped for good, and all around, the land seemed to go quiet.

Far off, the bell in the church steeple at the town common begin to chime. It sounded peaceful and ordinary. I thought of Grandma attending her meeting there, and of Grandpa back at the house, escorting patients into his office.

"You again? We've got to stop meeting like this," he'd tell the old ladies. It always got a laugh.

For some reason, my father came into my mind, and I almost got a clear sight of him in the cockpit of his plane, flying over France. But I was too excited about the guns to concentrate and he got away again.

I began counting with the chimes in a whisper. Carolyn raised up for a view and joined in. We whispered together, all eyes on the guns.

"Four ... five ... six ... seven ..."

On the eighth chime, a huge tongue of fire erupted out the end of the first gun. Then came a roar so loud that I felt as if my brain had exploded in my head. I saw a bird dropping straight down out of the sky, from shock it must have been. A moment later, the first echo of the concussion returned from across the water. It was so loud itself I thought for a minute that someone had fired back.

The second gun followed a few seconds later, and this time I saw how the flaming tongue reached almost to the beach embankment in front of it. The field blazed up and began to burn in places.

The sock of this explosion felt like a real body blow. Up and down the coast, great masses of birds flushed into the sky. I stood up and saw gulls, crows, ducks, terns and, from the inland ponds, Canada geese and even pure white swans flapping wildly upwind. The echoes from both blasts began to come back, again and again. They got mixed up with the ringing in my own ears until I couldn't tell which was which, and wondered if I was going deaf.

Somehow, underneath all this, I heard a whimper. I looked down and saw Carolyn curled into ball in the long grass. Her hands were gripping the sides of her head.

I dropped beside her and spoke to her, but she couldn't answer. She was trembling all over, her little body clenched up like a fist. There was nothing I could do to help her.

After a minute, she sat up, though, and took some deep gulps of air. Finally, she gave me a weak smile.

"I wasn't afraid!" she announced.

"You are very brave," I said. I really did think so, too.

"I didn't think it would be so loud."

"You aren't the only one." I held out my hand and showed her. I couldn't hold it still for anything.

Behind us, a commotion suddenly broke out.

"Carolyn, get down!" I said in her ear.

We ducked. Across the field, heading directly for us, came Abel Hoffman. He ran past about two yards away and I thought he hadn't seen us until he stopped at the edge of embankment just beyond our hiding place, turned back and glanced straight into our faces.

I froze. Beside me Carolyn went stiff. He stared at us with his mouth hung open, gasping for air, then he spun around and took a tremendous leap off the embankment. We heard his heavy grunt when he landed, knapsack and all, on the sand at the bottom. We stood up and crept closer to the edge where we could watch him. He was running like a madman up the beach. When he came to the wire fence, he slid through the slit and never stopped to put the dead brush back where it should go. He just ran on and on, and he was still running when he went around a curve in the shore and disappeared.

But that wasn't all Carolyn and I saw that day. Soon after, four soldiers with guns entered our field and began walking around the place where Abel had been standing. We got down fast. In a minute, someone gave a shout and I looked and saw a soldier holding up a blue cap.

"Spread out and search the field," another soldier yelled.

After this, my heart began to thud in my ears and I didn't look over the grass anymore, but lay flat and still and told Carolyn to lie still, too. We lay for what felt like hours, barely breathing, while boots tramped by on all sides. Every minute it seemed like the next minute we'd be caught.

10

THE TRAMPING DIED away. The field turned quiet. I thought it might be a trap and we lay still a while longer, straining our ears. The waves were rattling stones back and forth on the beach, making it hard to hear. Finally I peered above the grass. The soldiers were gone.

"Run," I told Carolyn. We slid down the embankment and took off along the beach. Not until we came out on the road did we slow down and have enough breath to talk.

"What if they'd found us?" Carolyn panted. "Would they put us in jail?"

"I don't know. I don't think so."

"Who was that man?"

"The German who lives in the woods. He shouldn't have been there. He knew it, too."

"Was he spying?"

I told her I didn't know for sure, that he might have been, but not to say anything to anyone yet.

"Well, he saw us," Carolyn said.

"I know he did."

"Will he do anything?"

"Probably not. He'll be too scared."

"I was scared," Carolyn said with a shudder. "I was scareder than I ever was."

"Well, keep quiet about it until I figure things out. And don't tell Mom no matter what. We'll get skinned."

After we got home, I tried to think of what to do. Abel Hoffman was looking worse and worse. You could tell by the way he was standing in the field that he wasn't there for fun. He was watching things too closely, first the guns, then the bay. Also he kept bending over to write in something— his notebook probably, the one he'd had on the day the guns came down the road.

I was ready to swear he was up to something, but I didn't want to raise a flap without being sure. I decided to tell El-liot first, and see what he thought. Maybe he'd noticed Abel doing something fishy at his boat-studio lately. After that, we might want to tell Uncle Jake, who could get word to someone at the fort quietly, without my mother finding out.

But when I took Carolyn back up to Grandma after lunch, Elliot was nowhere around.

"He hasn't come back yet. He's off looking for eggs," Grandma said.

I knew what that meant and headed home before she could think of some job I had to do. When I went up there for supper, he was back, but he was in one of his moods, and wouldn't even look at me. I knew I'd see him the next morning working on the hen houses, and thought I'd talk to him then. But that night at our cottage an officer from the fort knocked on the door. In his hand he held two small clumps of ear cotton.

Carolyn took one look and burst into tears. She ran for cover behind my mother.

"What is this? What is this?" my mother asked her in amazement. Carolyn would never cry just for a stranger at the door.

"I'm afraid I'll have to ask your boy some questions," the officer said. "We understand he was down near the guns with his sister this morning, watching the practice firing. There was someone else in that field. I'd like to ask him about it, if you don't mind."

And so we were caught after all. Carolyn's cotton wads had been found in the field during a second search. The soldier who'd passed us on his bicycle remembered her with the stuff sticking out of her ears. A few questions to neighbors and we'd been tracked down.

In a very short time, the officer, a lieutenant in charge of fort security, pried out of me everything I knew about our morning in the field, and also some things I hadn't known I'd known.

"This man, this supposed painter, had binoculars, you say? Big ones, small ones?"

"Big ones. He always has them, wherever he goes."

"So, high-powered binoculars." He wrote it down in a small book. "And a camera? Did he have a camera?"

"No."

"But he was observing the guns?"

"Yes."

"Anything else?"

"He'd look out to sea sometimes."

"With the binoculars? Did you think that was strange?"

"Yes."

"Was anything out there, in the bay, I mean?"

"No."

"Could he have been noting a direction, for instance the possible trajectory of shells?"

"I guess so."

"So, he was observing technical matters," the officer said, writing in his book.

"Maybe."

"Interesting."

My mother sat appalled and silent, holding Carolyn on her lap as if she were a little child again. The lieutenant smiled at her.

"Mrs. Saunders, you musn't think your children were in any danger. We had patrols monitoring the dangerous sections of beach. We anticipated trespassers. These two weren't the only ones out there, by any means. A good number of townsfolk slipped in to catch a glimpse, quite understandable under the circumstances. It's not every day a gun like that gets fired. Don't be too hard on your youngsters."

He gave me a wink and grinned at Carolyn, as if he would have done the same thing in our shoes. "We believe, however, that there may be those among us who have other motives than innocent spectating."

"The German painter in the woods?" my mother asked.

"I'm not the one to say about that. There's an agency man, FBI, who'll be coming down from Providence tonight."

"FBI!" I cried.

"Espionage is a federal offense," the lieutenant said. He glanced at my mother. "This is only a preliminary investigation, but it must remain confidential for the time being. Please, we ask that you not speak to anyone about what your son saw, or my visit this evening. This is very important."

"Of course."

"And Robert." He gazed at me. "We appreciate your honesty. We'd more or less guessed it was Hoffman from the blue cap we found out there. He's been under surveillance. We just needed confirmation."

"Has he done something else?"

"That's what we're checking into."

When the lieutenant stood up to go, I remembered the other thing I'd seen Abel Hoffman do in the field.

"I forgot to say, he had a notebook."

"A notebook?" The lieutenant swung around.

"He was writing in it. Or drawing, I couldn't really see. He could have been sketching the layout of the fort."

"Interesting. But he had no camera. You're sure?"

"Yes."

The lieutenant made a last note of this, thanked us again and left. He'd hardly closed the door behind him when my mother let go of Carolyn and turned furious eyes on me.

The lieutenant had said the investigation would be confidential but somehow, in the next twenty-four hours, almost everyone in town heard about it.

They heard Abel Hoffman had been in the field with binoculars and that he'd run off when an army patrol caught sight of him. They knew about his cap being found, about the slit in the fence, about his habit of going to the beach to paint.

The only thing they didn't know was that I was the one who'd talked. The fort took credit for uncovering everything and I was glad. I knew Abel had seen me and it made me nervous. But more than that, I was glad I hadn't told Elliot what I'd seen in the field. I'd never tell him now. If Elliot ever found out, he'd guess in a minute that I was the one who'd turned Abel in. For that, he'd never forgive me.

Sometime during the night, Abel was picked up at his boat-studio and brought down to the town hall for questioning. I heard about it when I went up to Grandma's the next morning. The news was all over town. The only thing I wanted to do was get into town myself to see what was happening. I worked on the hen houses, chopped some wood and set off as soon as I could. Elliot wasn't around. He was sick, Grandma said. I guessed that meant he'd heard the news, too.

People were crowding the commons, talking about Abel's arrest when I got there. The word had gone out that federal agents were in on the case and everyone had a theory of what that meant. Little groups were standing around in different places, then folks would go off to do a job or have a sandwich, and come back and join a new group. There was a feeling in the air of something big about to blow wide open. I saw some kids from my class at school and we horsed around together. I wondered what they would have thought if they knew I was the one who'd turned Abel in. I wanted to tell them but I kept quiet. The funny thing was, I wasn't sure myself what I'd seen Abel doing in that field. That's why I was there in town, milling around with everybody else. I was waiting to get told.

The police brought Abel out of the town hall about mid-afternoon. He looked jumpy and hollow-eyed. I was standing pretty far back in the crowd where it wasn't likely he'd see me. Just in case, though, I turned my face away and kind of watched slant-wise. Something was different about him. After a few seconds, I realized that he didn't have his boots on. The FBI agents hadn't let him put them on when they arrested him, or they'd grabbed him so fast that no one thought of it. He was walking around like a kid in his bare feet, hobbling over the gravel to get to the police car. It kind of took away the foreign look he'd always had for me before, made him look more ordinary.

When they got him in the car, he was driven away, not up to Providence as everyone thought, but to a place down the road where he was turned free and allowed to go back to the woods. Later, we found out he'd been released for lack of evidence, fined twenty-five dollars for trespassing on military property and warned against doing it again.

The FBI hadn't wanted to rile up the crowd around town hall by letting him loose on the spot. They were worried about Abel getting home in one piece. And they were right. A lot of people were mad when they found out. A rumor went around that the reason he got off so easy was a big-name friend of his in the art world in New York City had covered for him. Everybody thought the federal agents had fallen down on the job.

At supper that night, Grandpa said, "The man's hiding something, I can smell it. When somebody has to secret himself away in the woods like that, whether they're German or Pekingese, you know they're up to something." Though he'd taken in and treated Abel, he wasn't any more in favor of him than the rest of the town.

"I heard the police searched all over his place and

couldn't find anything," Aunt Nan said. "They were looking for a camera. That would have given them grounds to
remove him. They want him to get out but they can't make
him go without evidence. He has identification papers, all
proper and legal. Also he's on somebody's private land who
said he could be there."

"On whose?" Grandpa said. "That's who they should
arrest.

"Agnes Gunderson," said Aunt Nan, looking over at
Grandma. Grandpa looked over, too, because Agnes was
one of Grandma's dear friends. They did the flowers together at the church.

"Well, can't you talk some sense into the woman?"
Grandpa said to Grandma. "Does she even know he's
there?"

"She knows and she's in favor of it," Grandma said.
"Agnes isn't one to put a poor struggling artist out."

"Poor struggling artist!" Grandpa just about came out
of his suspenders. "He's the first poor struggling artist I
ever saw with a pair of fancy two-hundred dollar German
binoculars in a brand new leather case."

"Who says he has something like that?" Grandma asked.

"I say it!" Grandpa thundered. "I saw them with my
own eyes when he came to see me."

"He came to see you?" Grandma said in surprise.

"He did, for an injury, and I'm not going to say any
more about it," he barked out, as if he was afraid someone
might accuse him of aiding the enemy.

Uncle Jake came in then and the conversation swung around to the rubber shortage. He'd been up the lane helping old Mrs. Taylor change a flat on her Buick. It was the same tire that had gone two weeks ago, and a couple of weeks before that. She'd have to get it patched up again, too, because no way would she find a brand new tire these days, even if she could afford one.

"Guess you'll be up there again in another two weeks," Grandma said to Jake.

"Guess I will," he said, sitting down heavily.

We laughed, but my mind had gone back to the discussion about Abel Hoffman before. That was an interesting point Grandpa made about Abel's expensive binoculars. It kind of raised my suspicions about the man again. I wished I could tell Elliot about seeing Abel in the field to find out what he thought. But I couldn't, and besides, Elliot was upstairs having a bowl of soup in bed, not talking to anybody.

Without Elliot, I'd started playing baseball in the afternoons when my jobs around the house were done. A bunch of us were out hitting flies in the field beside the school when Abel came in to town for groceries and supplies one day about a week after he was arrested. He was taking dirty looks from almost everyone he passed. People were crossing the street to keep away from him. When Larry Bean from the filling station saw him heading for the post office, he yelled:

"Hey, it's the Nazi. Picking up your instructions, Nazi?"

We saw Abel look around and walk away fast. Then somebody, not one of us, threw a Coke bottle and it smashed to pieces on the street in front of him. He jumped like a spooked cat and ran up the steps to the post office, slamming the door after him. We all laughed. He looked so ridiculous.

While he was inside, Jerry Antler and Willie Vogel began to joke around about the way Abel talked. Willie was the kid whose dad had been killed in action, and he'd been getting kind of loud and sassy lately. He and Jerry had a little routine they'd worked up together after they'd over-heard Abel in the post office one time. Abel was in there almost every week to pick up packages. He ordered painting supplies from somewhere and had them shipped to him. A whole stream of stuff was always coming in from Boston or New York. No one could figure out where he got the money to buy it.

"Have-ensee post most wery please?" Willie would ask.

"What, not post?" Jerry would say. "Where what not post?"

Willie: "How where not post what?"

Jerry: "What not post commen where tomorrow, wery please?"

This would go on for a while, until everyone was practically on the ground laughing, which was how Abel found us when he came out that afternoon. He looked over and stared for a long second, then started away toward the grocery store.

I was laughing as hard as anyone, but when Abel

stopped and stared that way, I quit and turned my back on him fast.

"What's that matter with you? You look like you saw a ghost," Jerry told me.

I didn't say anything, but five minutes later I got out of there and went home. I thought Abel had seen me, had picked me out specially from everyone else there and given me a look. It made me wonder if the FBI agents had told him who talked, and I didn't want to be around when he came back down the road with his groceries.

Grandpa must have heard from one of his patients about the bottle-throwing incident because that night, he sounded off at the supper table.

"The fellow's a magnet for trouble. Arrest him on some charge, any charge, and get him out of here, that's what I say. By the time the FBI digs up enough evidence to prove anything, he'll have done whatever damage he's capable of, or it'll have been done to him."

"Now, Harvey," Grandma said. "There's nothing to prove the poor man's doing anything wrong." She was still siding with her friend Agnes.

"He's doing wrong just by living here!" Grandpa said. "It's bad enough that he's one of those crackpot artists. Freeloaders, every one of them, Communists and kooks."

Across the table, I saw Elliot begin to chew on his hand. He was downstairs eating with us again, though he still didn't look well.

"On top of that, what's he think?" Grandpa went on.

"That people around here aren't going to suspect a Kraut? We're at war with them, for pity's sake. Why is he here, on this coast, right next to our military installations? That's what I want to know. If he's what he says he is, why isn't he painting his rubbish in Kansas . . . or Ohio," Grandpa turned to look accusingly at me, "where he doesn't pose a risk? Anyone would think he was up to something. Maybe he is and maybe he isn't, but the man's asking for trouble. He's going to get it, too."

The dark, twisted look that came over Elliot's face while he listened to this made me feel sick myself. I couldn't stand to see him hurt, even when I thought he was wrong. I saw how he hated Grandpa for the things he said, and at the same time, how he wouldn't allow himself to fight back, no matter what. I'd never known anyone like that and it really stumped me. If I could have stood up for Elliot, I would have. That night I almost did anyway. But Grandpa was right about Abel being a magnet for trouble. He was right about Abel asking for it by staying around.

After supper, I went up to Elliot's room, which I hadn't done for a while. He took this as a kind peace sign and showed me a wild turkey egg he'd found. Wild turkey eggs were rare around Sachem's Head, as rare as wild turkeys themselves, so this was a real find.

"What are you going to do with your egg collection when you've found every egg there is? Sell it for a million dollars?" I asked him, kind of half-kidding.

"Well, first of all I'll never find every egg," he said.

"But what if you did?"

"I'd never sell it," Elliot said. "I'd never give it away to a museum or anything either. I'd just keep it and have it to go over whenever I wanted. Every single egg that's here, I know where I found it and how and when, so it's special. If I gave them away, no one would know anything about them. They'd just be this mass of old birds' eggs that people came to see because they were all together in one place. What good would that do?"

I don't know why, but I loved that answer. I looked at Elliot and just shook my head. It seemed to me that no one else in the world or in the history of the world would have thought that way about a dumb egg collection. Elliot was the only one.

A few minutes later, though, he brought the conversation around to a place I wished he wouldn't.

"I was at Abel's today," he said. "He's afraid to go into town, now."

"Well, he should be afraid," I couldn't help saying.

"He doesn't dare go anywhere to paint, not even the beaches that are open," Elliot said. "He stays in the woods."

"Sounds like a smart idea. You know, if I were him, I might start thinking of other places to live."

Elliot shook his head. "He can't leave now. You should see what he's doing. Big oils, six feet across, that make it look like the sea is going to rise up and break through the surface."

"Hm-mm."

"He says they're going to make his name over here. Listen, Robert, you should come look. Abel's been really good lately. No drinking, just work. He's a really nice man underneath. If people knew him, they'd get to love him. That's why all of this is so stupid."

"He should start learning better English."

"He is!" Eliott said. "I'm helping him. And he's helping me a little with . . . with my stuff, you know. He thinks I'm coming along okay."

"When he bothers to pay attention to you."

"He does! Not every minute, but I wouldn't expect that."

"Once a month?" I asked meanly.

Elliot glanced at me angrily.

"I'll show you," he said. "This is what I'm doing now."

He drew out a pile of paintings from under his bed and brought them over to his table. They were all done with oil paint and he was very proud of them. While I looked through them, I could hear him almost holding his breath with excitement.

I'd always been in awe of Elliot's talent but these new things were terrible. They were supposedly country scenes, but the trees in them didn't look like trees, more like crazed jellyfish. There was a brook that was just a purple line, when he used to be able to draw every bubble and stone. He'd painted a picture of Abel in front of his boat. You couldn't tell that from looking at it though. I had to ask what it was.

"I'm painting appearances," Elliot said. "Not objects so

much as the way they appear in different lights, at different times of day."

"The sky in this painting is yellow. Abel is a pink lump."

"Right. The sun is in my eye."

"But how is a person supposed to know that?"

"It doesn't matter. Why do you have to know exactly what everything is? Maybe it's better not to know."

"How is it better?"

"It makes you see things differently, not just the same old way you think they should look."

I couldn't understand this at all, which made him mad. Then I got angry and told him he was wasting his talent. The next minute, he ordered me out of his room, and we were back to being sore at each other.

Nothing that had happened to Abel made any difference to Elliot. He kept on going to the woods to paint. Most afternoons he was there. On Sundays, when Grandma gave us the day off from chores, he went over in the morning and stayed until supper. He was secretive about it, I'll say that for him. I don't think people in town had any more idea than his own family what he was doing. He might even have got away with it if he'd kept up that way. But he didn't. He made a mistake. He started running errands for Abel.

The Coke bottle had put Abel into a permanent state of fright. Afterwards, he never wanted to go into town again, and with Elliot there, he didn't have to. At first Elliot was just buying a few groceries for him. For all anyone knew, they were for his own mother or his grandmother. Later, Abel began to send him for his mail and the packages of supplies he needed to keep painting. The post office staff took note of this and word went around, very quietly, that Elliot Marks was doing jobs for the German in the woods. I heard it from the kids I played ball with, and talked it down the best I could. You can set a rumor against a rumor and have it work for a while.

Sachem's Head being a small village, no one spoke to Aunt Nan or Grandma about Elliot. I guess people felt it would have seemed impolite, as if Aunt Nan and Grandma didn't know their own business. Nobody told Grandpa, either, or even Uncle Jake. Elliot went on doing Abel's errands, and people went on watching him, and nothing seemed to come of it. All during the second half of July this continued, until even I stopped worrying and began to think everything would work out all right.

Partly, it was the weather. The days had turned hot and clear. The smell of ripe field grass drifted in the air. Practice air-raid sirens still went off, searchlights patrolled the sky at night, in Europe and the Pacific the fighting went on but, for a little while, the war let go its grip on our lives.

Carolyn went to the beach every day with a family up the road. My mother and Aunt Nan took some time off from work. Grandpa and Grandma rolled up their sleeves and gardened side-by-side in the long evenings, "happy as two old peas," Grandma said.

"This is what carries us over the rough spots," I heard her telling Aunt Nan. "Thank heaven for summer in Sachem's Head."

I was in good spirits, too, and played a lot of baseball. Even Elliot was happy; happier than I'd ever seen him and maybe than he'd ever been. He went around the house in the same shadowy way he always had, avoiding Grandpa when he could, but he spent less time in his room, and his hand-chewing disappeared. His skin tanned until it looked almost healthy. When we worked together for Grandma, we could joke around as long as we stayed off the subject of Abel Hoffman.

It wasn't easy to tiptoe around Abel, though, not for either of us. I could see Elliot wanted to talk about what he was learning. He'd come home practically bursting sometimes, and half of me would want to ask about it, but the other half was against Abel, and afraid of him, and didn't want to know anything good about him. Everybody in town was waiting for the German to make a false move. I was waiting, too, though Elliot didn't know it. I told myself it was my duty to keep an eye out. My country might depend on it. But I was scared all the time. I worried what would happen to Elliot if Abel was caught spying again. I worried what would happen if I was the one who caught him.

Luckily, Abel was deep in his woods, far out of sight.

Three weeks went by and nobody heard anything about him. You could almost begin to believe he wasn't there anymore, except that Elliot went to the woods and came back, went and came back. He had his own knapsack, now. Grandma and Aunt Nan thought it was for his birds' egg collection. I knew better.

One morning while we were working our stint in the vegetable garden, weeding out the carrots and string beans and, this being August, tying up the tomatoes that were just beginning to ripen, Elliot asked me to come to Abel's with him. He asked me for that afternoon, said Abel had a lot of new stuff to see. I shouldn't miss it.

I looked over at him and didn't know what to say. All sorts of suspicions went through my head about why he was asking me, and even what Abel might be up to.

"Does Abel know you're inviting me?" I asked finally.

"He says it's fine. You can come any time. He remembers that you liked his painting."

I laughed. We both knew that was a lie.

"Has Abel said anything about me lately?"

"I don't think so. He's been too busy to think about people. Why?"

"I just wondered."

"So you'll come?"

"Are you sure you really want me to?"

"If you don't, you'll be missing out," Elliot said. "I think you'll like what he's doing now."

I saw that this was really about art, nothing else, and I said I would go. It gave me a good feeling to know that Elliot would trust me to come see Abel's paintings again. Maybe, with all the work he'd been doing, Abel had forgotten who I was. Or maybe he never had recognized me, and the strange stare he'd given me at the post office hadn't meant anything. I didn't really believe that, but I decided to go anyway. I wanted to have another look at Abel Hoffman.

We went over after lunch. Some pilots from the Quonset Air Station were practicing dropping fire bombs in the bay and there was a terrific racket going on the whole time we were walking. Their planes were navy dive bombers with dipped wings and we watched them go up high in formation, then sweep down and come in low, one by one, over the water.

We could see the bombs drop out of their bellies, but we weren't close enough to the bay to see the explosions when the bombs hit the water. We could hear them, though, big tearing roars that made you think of what they could be blowing up instead of just sea water.

"How's your father doing?" Elliot asked.

"He's okay. A lot of American flyers are over there now with him. They want to do daytime bombing runs so they can target better, but the Brits don't like getting shot up. They only want to fly at night."

"I hope he'll be all right," Elliot said. "Then when he comes back, maybe he'll come here."

"Don't count on it," I said. "My mother didn't even want to tell him we were here. She only wrote him the truth about a month ago."

"Why?"

"She thought he wouldn't like it. He didn't either. We just heard from him. He wants us to go back to the farm as soon as we can."

Elliot nodded, as if he understood. "I've never met your dad," he said. "I wish he'd come here just for a little while so I could meet him. He has a bad leg, doesn't he?"

"Always has," I said. "From a flying accident way back when he was doing mail runs."

"Is that what he says did it?"

"Well, yes. Was there something else you heard?"

Elliot shook his head and wouldn't say any more. I knew not to hound him. I was curious, though, why he'd said that, and put it into the back of my mind, along with the other scraps of clues I'd picked up about my father in Sachem's Head.

A few minutes later, we came up on Abel Hoffman's boat-studio in the field. He was standing in front of an easel, painting away, and paintings were lying all around him on the grass. Others were stacked against the side of the boat, or set up against trees or bushes. Since I'd last been there, Abel had built himself another, much bigger, shed off to the side of the first one. Inside it, I saw a lot more paintings leaning up against each other.

"Look at all this stuff. He's been really working!"

"That's what I've been telling you," Elliot said in a low voice as we crossed the field. "He hates to stop. As soon as he finishes one he goes right on to the next, as if he's afraid it won't get done otherwise. But he's happy. He's happy most of the time."

Something I'd noticed about Abel when I was there before was how much energy he put into his painting. He wasn't the kind of painter that stands quietly in one spot dabbing here and there. Whatever he was working on, he was all over the place, running around it, standing back from it, rushing in for some big swipes with the brush then moving away again.

Abel probably used up as much energy painting as most people do playing sports or hiking up a mountain. That afternoon, when we came up, he was going full blast on the job, and he didn't notice for a while that we were there. But finally his eye fell on Elliot, and he gave him a big shout, and lifted his brush to me, too.

"Come! Look! I paint the planes. Do you hear?"

We listened, and heard the bombing still going on in the bay. "Yah?" Abel's eyes widened and he leapt toward the canvas he was working on.

"Bomb, here!" He made a movement with his brush that put an explosion of paint on the painting. "And here!" Another paint explosion. "And here, here, here!"

He was using different shades of red and blue, sort of layering them together, and though the explosions he painted didn't look like anything recognizable, I saw the power that went into them, the thick blue craters of paint his brush left behind.

"That's great!" Elliot told him. For the first time, I agreed.

"Yah! Great!" Abel said. "I am great again!" He gave a scornful laugh. "In Germany, I am great, and kablam!" He exploded his brush against the canvas. "Is gone."

"You mean a bomb fell on your paintings?" I asked.

"Bomb?" Abel glanced at me. "Not like this." We listened to the navy pilots practicing over the bay.

"Another bomb. Big. Smart. You don't see at first. You think: Oh, this is nothing, it won't catch me. Suddenly, you can't do nothing. It starves you out, beats you out, comes after you. You hide. And still it comes. It finds what you paint before and this also it destroys. So there is nothing left. Just you. Then if you don't leave, it will get that, too."

"So you left?" Elliot asked.

"I get out," Abel said, in a low voice. "For many, it is too late."

"Tell us," Elliot said, and I could see it was something he'd asked before. "Please, Abel. Tell us what happened. We should know."

"You should NOT KNOW!" Abel said angrily. "Who should know such things? Not children."

"Yes, we should," Elliot pleaded. "In case it happens again. Here, even. We should know when to leave."

When Elliot said this, Abel dropped his brush and ran his large, paint-smeared hands through his hair.

"This is true," he said, and sat down heavily where he was on the grass.

11

LISTENING TO ABEL was like watching him paint.

"In old days, I have in Germany, many, many friends!" he bellowed. "We are young, poor, full with ideas! "

Then he whispered: "Where are they now, these talented ones? Hiding, like me. Arrested. Or worse, dead."

He leapt up suddenly and threw his arms in the air: "What to do! How to fight? Everywhere is evil now!"

He sat again, glaring into space while he made the next sentence in his mind.

In this way, we learned how, long before the war, he left his family's home in Berlin to go to an art school in the city of Frankfurt. There he met other young artists experimenting in ways he had never imagined possible. No longer was it good enough to draw, line by line, the simple appearance of things. Now one must learn to paint the invisible: hidden feelings and memories, terrors and passions, the submerged continents everyone knows are there but cannot speak about.

He began his own experiments.

"I wanted my paintings to roar!" he shouted to us. "To roar and . . . and . . . what is that called in the ocean?" he asked Elliot, nodding toward the naval practice runs.

"Explosions? To explode?"

"Yah, to explode. To make a big sound. But also to make silence. And quiet, like water dripping after a storm. A painting can do many things. It can make the eye hear."

In Germany, his work began to be noticed. Expressionist, it was called. He used paint straight from the tube. Pure colors. A tube of paint is like a stick of dynamite, he said. The surface of things is exploded. Inner landscapes are revealed.

Younger painters came and lived near him. He gained a reputation, supported himself comfortably, though he was never rich. He lived in city apartments, moved about to Munich, to Dresden, to Paris for a year, then home to Frankfurt, where he was appointed to a professor's post at the famous Art Academy.

But a new political order was growing in Germany. The Nazi Party came to power in 1933. Hitler and his circle disliked the new art. It looked crazy they said, as if mental patients had painted it. Good art does not try to confuse people or disgust them. It is clear and vigorous, straightforward and beautiful, and provides the public with uplifting subjects, natural landscapes and scenes of normal life.

Well, all right. Everyone is entitled to his or her own

opinion. There is room for all kinds of art, all kinds of opinions in the world.

Except with Hitler, there was to be only one room, Abel Hoffman told us. Very soon, he and his brutish regime began to eliminate the other rooms. How? This is how.

A letter arrives from the new chairman of the art department. You are dismissed from your professorship at the Art Academy. The money for your post has been cut off. You must leave immediately, after ten years! Why? You have been judged an unfit artist, one of the degenerates who are trying to fool people, or corrupt them. When you go to interview for another teaching job, you are turned away. Your name is on a list. No one will hire you.

You find work painting wall decorations in office buildings. It's demeaning and physically exhausting, but helps pay the bills. You work on your own art, too, but sell less and less.

One night, a knock comes on the door. It's the police, Hitler's dreaded Gestapo, accompanied by your landlord, wringing his hands.

—Are you Hoffman?

—Yes.

—You must leave at once. This apartment is needed by the state.

—But where can I go?

—That's your problem. What is this trash on the floor, your paintings?

—Yes.

—We must confiscate them.

—Why?

—We're under orders.

—But, where will you take them?

—We'll let you know.

The paintings, your newest and best, are carried away. They disappear. No one will tell you where they are. You move in with a friend. Before long, you're fired from your wall painting job. Why? You're one of those blacklisted artists. Your employer has a business to protect. You are too risky.

You are officially notified that your work has been declared "obscene" and anti-German in spirit. The government has ordered it removed from museums and public places. It cannot be sold. Dealers will be prosecuted. "But I paint nature!" you cry. "You have deformed nature," comes the reply.

One night, in the town square, a huge bonfire is lit for the enjoyment of the people. The fuel is books, furniture, musical manuscripts, Parisian hats, paintings, photographs, and masses of indistiguishable junk. In the fire, the painter catches sight of a pile of his canvases just beginning to ignite. There's the one he painted in Dresden, of the bridge and the birds feeding below in the snow. He never wanted to sell it because it reminded him of himself that winter. Solitary, cold, his young followers pecking for crumbs nearby.

The painter hurls himself toward the fire. He tries to rescue his work but is dragged back by several people in the crowd. Is he crazy? Does he want to kill himself? He stares at the flames in shock. The paint on his painting begins to melt and char. He turns away in tears, runs his hands through his hair. He can't bear to watch.

After this, the painter becomes more secretive about his art. He moves out of town to a nondescript house in the suburbs. He paints in the cellar, warns friends to come only after dark, talks to no one in the neighborhood. No one knows who or what he is.

His ex-students drop in for visits. They're young and angry and make plans to get around the stupid Nazi laws. They organize secret exhibitions, print underground articles and newspapers. The year is 1935 and it's exciting at first. The painter's cellar becomes subversively famous. Silently, the neighbors take note of the comings and goings.

One evening, walking home from his job in a local canning factory, the painter is jumped and beaten by a gang of thugs. Get out of this neighborhood, they tell him. Degenerate artists are not wanted here. They smash his stomach and kidneys with their fists and slam his head over and over into a roadside curbstone. He vomits, passes out, and wakes up a few minutes later with a crowd of people around him. They have been told he is a drunk who has passed out on his way home from a bar.

In fact, he stinks of liquor. Someone has poured a bottle

of whiskey over him. Depraved pig, get out, this is a nice neighborhood, the crowd shrieks at him. He gets unsteadily to his feet and drags himself back to his cellar.

The shock of the assault unhinges him. Some of his ex-students have been badly beaten as well. The meetings in the cellar stop. Eyes are everywhere. He's afraid to go out and can no longer work in the canning factory. He's plagued by nightmares. For the first time, he feels afraid for his life. With the help of friends, he moves to a new apartment in a new town.

But here, somehow, the Gestapo knows him, is on the look-out for him. He cannot buy art supplies, meet people, go anywhere, without being watched. At unexpected times during the day or night, Gestapo agents arrive at his apartment. They search for paintings and even check to see if his brushes are wet.

One evening, he is arrested and taken to Gestapo headquarters. He has been denounced for making comments critical of the government. Who is the informer? Another painter, a colleague, someone he thought he could trust. Fortunately, after a long interrogation, the charges are dropped for lack of evidence.

The painter goes home exhausted. He thinks angrily: Turned in by a colleague! How could he have done it? Then his anger fades. He knows how. Everyone is afraid. No one is trustworthy when fear rules a house.

During the next two years, the painter works as a street

sweeper, a flower delivery man, and a dishwasher in a restaurant, but is fired from each of these jobs for illness. His health is beginning to fail.

With his landlord's permission, he paints at night in an unheated bathroom at the back of the house, using watercolors to avoid the smell of oil paint. But he dares sell nothing. The police are watching, waiting for him to make a move so they can arrest him again.

He does not have enough food and faints on the street one winter day.

Two well-known Expressionist artists, friends of his, have committed suicide, he hears. Another has been deported to a concentration camp. The daily outrages committed against the Jews sicken him. A friend tells him: leave Germany before it's too late. Worse is coming. We are going to war.

He is penniless. Where can he go?

One day, he collapses in an outdoor market and ends up in the hospital. His heart has gone bad. While he is hospitalized, his landlord and family are arrested and deported to a concentration camp, for what it's never clear. The house, with all the painter's possessions inside, is boarded up.

A former student who is in town, comes to see him in his hospital room and is shocked to find his old teacher in such a weakened state. Get yourself out of here before it's too late, he says. If they arrest you again, you won't last a month. He hands over his own train ticket for Geneva. The student will buy another ticket in third class, and accompany him. There are people in Switzerland who can help get the painter out. To Spain. From there, he can get a boat to America, the student says.

America! How can I go there? I don't speak any English, the painter cries.

He goes the next day, telling no one, leaving everything, even his secret watercolors, which lie under a floorboard in the cold bathroom. He sets out with only the clothes on his back, just in time, he finds out later.

Gestapo agents searching his old rented room have found letters linking him to an anti-government organization, exactly what they need to throw him into the camps. Arriving at the hospital to make his arrest, the agents find his bed empty.

"They missed you by a day," a friend writes from Germany several months later. "I wept with joy when they told me you had gone." It is his old colleague, the one who had turned him in.

Abel Hoffman stopped. He'd been talking for a long time. The sun was lower; its rays had ebbed as quietly as tide water across the field. Now only the top half of the trees on the other side were lit. There, perched on one branch, I saw Abel's loyal hawk keeping watch, his fierce, hooked beak turned a bit to one side.

At some time unnoticed, the bombing in the bay had

come to an end, and as Abel's voice broke off, a strange crater of silence opened around us. Abel's face wore a dazed look, as if telling his story had made him live it again and he wasn't sure that this time he had come out alive. After a little while, he got to his feet. When he'd walked off a ways, he turned back and gazed at me.

I looked away fast. I had no doubt by then that he knew I'd told on him being in the field. His story about the double-crossing colleague in Germany put me on notice that he'd dealt with spineless types like me before. I was pretty sure now he hadn't been spying, and I went hot with shame. When I looked again, though, he was examining his bomb painting. To Elliot, he said:

"You take this one. It is the best."

"You mean, this painting?" Elliot asked in amazement.

"Take it to home. Today. Two can carry."

"But Abel, why? It's much safer here. Anyway, I have no place to put it," Elliot protested. The painting was very large, six feet by six feet.

"Please," he said. "I wish to give to you some gift."

"We could put it in the barn," I said.

"We'd have to hide it," Elliot objected.

"Well, we could. There's a ton of stuff in there no one ever bothers with."

"Why are you giving it to me?" Elliot asked Abel suspiciously. "You're not thinking of leaving, are you?"

"No, no. I think of *staying*," Abel assured him. "How

can I leave?" He grinned and glanced over his shoulder.

We followed his eyes toward his two sheds packed tight with new paintings, his boat-studio moored in the field. It did seem impossible that he could go anywhere. The huge paintings alone would need a railroad boxcar to carry them, and we knew that Abel would never leave without them.

Elliot looked relieved. "I was afraid you might have decided to go," he said. "You know, without telling anyone, like in Germany."

"No, no." The painter shook his head. "No more. I am tired and . . ." he pressed his hand against his chest, "I feel not so good sometimes. For now, I stay."

Elliot nodded. "Your watercolor paintings might still be there under the floorboards. Maybe when the war is over you'll go back and find them."

"Maybe." Abel shrugged.

"And your other paintings in the museums. The Nazis couldn't burn everything, could they?"

"Now there is bombs," Abel said. "From the sky. In cities, many many bombs."

It was true. I thought how my father might be dropping a bomb that very minute headed for a building holding Abel's paintings. From the sky who could tell a museum from a weapons factory?

Maybe Abel was thinking that, too. He was staring again at his painting.

"Please, you take it," he urged Elliot. "Take it today."

"All right," Elliot agreed this time. "I'll take very good care of it."

"This I know," Abel said. "This I am sure. You ask why?" He turned to me. "This person, your cousin, is a painter. I know his heart. Inside him, I see. He paints good work someday. Not now. First he must learn. And work. Later, he is good. It is in his heart."

Elliot stared at the ground while Abel spoke. Afterwards, he walked away pretending to take an interest in Abel's hawk. I saw his eyes widening and narrowing, widening and narrowing at the hawk, who looked curiously back with an unblinking gaze.

A little while later we set out for home, carrying the painting upright between us. The canvas was still wet in places from the paint Abel had flung on that day. Rather than walk through the woods, we went a longer way across fields toward the bay, and by a back route along the shoreline. No one was around to see us, and though a few bugs flew into the wet paint, and Elliot tripped once and dropped his side in some tall grass, we came up behind the barn with Abel's painting still in one piece.

We leaned it against the outside wall, and went in for supper. Later, when it began to get dark, we took it around through the barn doors and hauled it to a high hayloft where no one else was likely to go.

"Stand it up. I'm going to stay and look at it," Elliot said, as I was about to lay the painting on the floor.

"Haven't you seen it enough by now?"

Elliot shook his head.

I climbed back down the ladder and waited, hoping he'd come. Outside, I heard my mother arrive home with Aunt Nan, and go in the house to pick up Carolyn. She came out and called for me, but I didn't want to go home yet, so I kept quiet. At last they went on without me.

When the barn got too dark to see more than vague shapes, I lit a kerosene lamp that was hanging on one of the old horse stalls, but Elliot still didn't come. Finally, I shouted up:

"Elliot, what are you doing?"

There was no answer.

"Elliot, I know why Abel gave you the painting. Don't you want to know?"

Silence . . . except from somewhere in the rafters, a snap and flutter of wings. Barn swallows, settling in for the night.

"Elliot!"

I heard him coming down, step by careful step. He got to the bottom and faced me.

"Abel's afraid, that's why he gave it to you," I said. "He's scared he's running out of time."

"You mean his heart?"

"Not that. Didn't you listen to what he said? Everything that happened to him in Germany is happening all over again here."

"It isn't the same."

"Why isn't it? He's getting beaten up. He's getting arrested. He's a magnet for trouble, just like he was there."

Elliot's eyes blinked fast in the lamplight. "You want him to leave like everybody else."

I shook my head. I did want him to leave, but not like everyone else. I'd changed my mind that afternoon.

"Abel doesn't fit in here. People are afraid of him," I told Elliot.

"They'll get used to him. His English is getting better. Anyway, they hardly see him anymore."

"They see him even when they don't see him. They're waiting, that's all. One little slip and they know they'll have him. He doesn't have a chance."

"You're on Grandpa's side, aren't you?" Elliot said in a hard, dry voice.

"No, I'm not. Not anymore. I'm on Abel's. You said it yourself, you have to know when to leave."

"Well, it's not time yet."

"Elliot, *anyone* can see it's time. Past time. If you really cared about Abel, you'd be telling him that instead of helping him stay around."

This made Elliot furious. He drew himself up as if he might hit me. To him, Abel's leaving was impossible. He couldn't stand even the thought of it.

"You keep away from him," he said, shakily. "And keep away from me, too. I'm not speaking to you anymore."

"Elliot, don't." I stepped toward him.

"Stay away!" Elliot shrieked. He shoved me back and ran out the barn door. I heard his feet pounding toward the house, and the outraged slam of a door.

I reached over and turned off the kerosene lamp. The dim outline of the barn door appeared and through it, the glimmer of a few stars. I walked out and just then, a great roar of planes came up on the house. A formation of five aircraft passed low overhead with a rush of dark metal.

They were headed to sea on a reconnaissance mission, an ordinary event. Maybe Elliot's anger had sharpened my senses because as their wing lights passed over, a cold fear went through me. I began to run home through the dark, remembering how my mother had called me, not once, but many times in the yard that night. Remembering a tremble in her voice, and how Carolyn had called out for me, too. I raced down the road, into the cottage driveway, across the front lawn. My mother heard my hand on the latch.

"Robert?"

She was getting up as I rushed in. The look on my face must have asked the question.

"It's your father," she said. "We've had a telegram. His plane's lost, shot down over the channel. They're out searching for him this very minute."

12

OVERNIGHT, IT SEEMED, I became an expert on battle news: Allied skirmishes against the Germans in North Africa, the German army's drive into Russia, the marines landing at Guadalcanal. I read the newspapers Grandpa left lying around and listened to the radio. The geography of Europe obsessed me. On a map I'd cut out of a magazine, I followed the action. I knew the locations of battles, the towns occupied, the likely position of airfields in England (no one knew where they were, exactly) and the flight routes of bombing raids. That was how I answered when people asked about my dad.

He was downed, not lost, we said. His whereabouts were "as yet unreported." The strain showed on my mother's face, which looked puffy and beat-up, as if she'd been in a fight. She stayed home from work, scared that news would come while she was away. Carolyn could make her cry by asking too many questions.

"Don't ask Mom anymore if they found him," I told her. "She can't stand being asked that."

"But I want to know!"

"She'll tell you when she finds out anything. Do you think she wouldn't tell you first thing?"

"But where is he?" Carolyn said. "Why can't they find him? They could go out in the ocean and find where the plane is and get him into a boat. Then he could come home."

"Maybe they will," I told her. "I hope they will. But don't tell Mom that stuff. She's too tired."

Grandpa said nothing about Dad, as usual, but Grandma opened up and talked about him. She came to visit us now, bringing casseroles and cookies. She ate lunches with my mother, helped splice together a clothes line that had snapped, made paper dolls with Carolyn. While she worked, she talked. She was the one who told us that Dad used to draw when he was a kid. She told us about a portrait he'd made of his dog, Baron, using colored pencils. The next time she came, she brought it over and it was pretty good. Not anything like Elliot could do, but okay. My mother said she had no idea my dad had a knack like that.

"Do you have anything else he did?" I asked.

"No, I wish I'd kept a few more. There was a year when he worked pretty hard at it. Then he gave up, I guess. Your Grandpa had him out hunting, fishing, building the hen houses out back. And there was his schoolwork to attend to. Your dad used to get behind. He didn't like studying, but the way our house worked, he'd have to get it done or he wasn't allowed to do anything else."

"Did you know that Elliot can draw?" I asked Grandma. "He's good, too. He just doesn't like to show people."

She nodded her head kind of sadly. "Elliot's another one who gets behind on his schoolwork," she said.

My father was still missing when, toward the middle of August, another convoy ship was torpedoed off Cape Cod. A day later, we heard that Abel Hoffman had been arrested again. The rumor went around that he'd been sneaking into houses near him and stealing food—an apple pie, a leg of lamb. It didn't sound much like Abel to me but, whatever was true, the charges were quickly upgraded when another search of his place in the woods uncovered a pile of drawings overlooked before.

They were detailed studies of the fort showing buildings, weapons sites, fortifications. People were shocked but not really surprised. The idea was about that Abel had played a part in the latest submarine attack.

He'd been in jail two days when Elliot showed up at our cottage one morning. I was in the backyard watering a few tomato plants I'd planted for my mother. I saw him coming, but didn't look up. Two weeks had passed since Elliot had pushed me in the barn and told me to stay away from him. In all that time, he'd never spoken to me, not even about my father being shot down. I was pretty burned up about it.

"They arrested Abel again, did you know?" he asked as he came up.

"I heard," I snapped out.

"Listen, I need you to help me. You know those drawings Abel supposedly did of the fort? They aren't his. They're the ones I drew. Remember? After we went through the fence that first time? I brought them over to show Abel and forgot to take them home."

I shrugged. "So go and tell somebody."

"I did tell them. They don't believe me."

"Who doesn't?"

"The FBI. They've sent three agents this time because they think Abel's case is so bad. They're interrogating him all the time, in shifts to try to break him down. Abel told them the drawings are works of art, by another artist. When they asked who, he wouldn't tell."

"So how did you find out?"

"Tony Wagner told me." His dad was a town policeman. "I went to the police station yesterday and said I was the one who drew the fort drawings. No one believed me. They basically said to shut up or I'd get in trouble."

"Sounds like good advice to me."

Elliot gave me a hard look.

"The FBI has been spying on Abel. All summer, probably. They knew I'd been there a lot."

"They didn't need a spy to figure that out. Everybody in town knew."

Elliot looked down at the tomato plants. "I don't care what people know."

"Well, I do. I'm not getting stuck in the middle of this. Abel should have left when he could. You should have made him go."

Elliot stood beside me, watching me water. After a minute, he said:

"Robert, it's awful what's happening. When the police brought Abel in, a big crowd of people stood outside the station and yelled at him, terrible things. They threw rocks and garbage at the door he went in. Yesterday, they were there doing it again. One man brought a live chicken and said its name was Nazi Hoffman. He threw it on the ground and let people kick it around for a while, then he grabbed it and wrung its neck. Everyone laughed. The police didn't do anything. They all want to kill him."

I looked up at last.

"Well, what should I do?"

"Come with me and back me up about the fort drawings. Please? You're the only one who knows I did them."

I walked over to the outside faucet and turned off the water. I coiled up the hose. Elliot watched. I wondered if he even knew what he was asking me to do.

"Robert, please."

"What makes you think the Feds are going to believe me any more than you? We're in the same family, you know."

"You weren't his friend."

"No, I'm your friend," I said angrily.

"Well, that doesn't matter so much," Elliot said.

That made me furious. I thought for a minute that I would tell him to get lost. "Sorry, Elliot, I don't have time," I'd say. "My father's been shot down, in case you forgot. Why would I stick out my neck for some dumb Kraut?"

Then I looked up again and knew I couldn't say that. The reason was, it was unfair what was happening to the man. However stupid he was to be living in our woods, however German he was, he was no spy. He didn't deserve to be arrested. Somebody had to stand up for him. Somebody had to take the heat or we might just as well have been living in Nazi Germany.

"Okay," I said to Elliot. "Let's go."

"Robert, thank you! You're a real, true friend."

I was still angry at him and didn't want to be thanked. "Don't worry," I said, "I'm not doing it for that."

We ran, and got to the town hall about 10 A.M. But the FBI agents had gone up to Providence the night before and weren't due back until noon.

"Stick around. I know they want to see *you* again," the police clerk said to Elliot when we went inside to ask. "You and your parents."

"My parents! Why?"

"You're all in big trouble, that's why. People who keep company with German spies can expect to have problems when they're found out."

"Who said anything about my parents?"

The clerk glanced away smugly. I could see from Elliot's face that his nerves were getting ready to act up so I dragged him outside.

"Why was she talking about my parents?" he whispered.

"She doesn't know anything. Don't get worked up about it."

"But, are people talking about my parents?"

"Probably. That's what people do."

Right then, for the first time I think, Elliot began to realize how actions he'd taken could spill over onto others, coloring how people felt about them. Up to then, he'd kept so apart from his family that he'd never thought of how he might be affecting them, only of how they affected him. I could see he was turning it over in his mind.

We stayed nearby waiting for noon, sitting on stone walls around the town common, walking through the old graveyard a couple of times. Some gravestones dated back to the early 1700s when the Indians were still in Sachem's Head, living down in the same woods where Abel's place was.

We bought a soda at the grocery store and took turns swigging it in front of the magazine rack. There were some good comic books for sale there.

"You should draw comics," I told Elliot. "You're as good as any of these guys."

"I used to try sometimes," Elliot answered. "The thing was, I could never think of anything funny."

"That's funny."

"What is?"

"Your funny unfunniness."

"My unfunny funnilessness, you mean?"

"See? You're getting funnier."

"Funny you should say that," Elliot said, with a gallows grin that made me smile just seeing it. The trouble with Elliot was, you couldn't stay mad at him very long, especially if he didn't want you to.

Ten minutes later, when we came out of the store, people were beginning to gather in front of the police station. We could see that something had happened. We went over and someone said the agents were back and they were going to take Abel up to the state prison outside of Providence.

"Right now?" Elliot asked.

"That's what they're saying."

"Why can't he stay here?"

"His own safety, probably. There's a lot of feeling against him in this town."

We stood off to one side and soon the station door swung open. Abel Hoffman stepped out between two police officers. He looked awful. His hair was matted and his clothes were rumpled. His face didn't have much expression on it. He stopped and blinked in the sunlight, then turned his head aside as if the brightness hurt his eyes. They'd cuffed his hands in front of him. When Elliot saw him like that, he made a strange noise, a kind of gurgle, and went into one of his freezes. Some loudmouths in the crowd began to yell.

"Hey Kraut, we got you this time."

"You've sunk your last ship, Nazi."

"You're dead meat now."

Nasty stuff, but Abel didn't look up. He shuffled forward, doing what he was told. There didn't seem to be any spirit left in him. The officers cleared a path through the crowd and led him out to the street where a black sedan waited. They were getting ready to put him in the backseat when an argument started up about his handcuffs. The Sachem's Head police didn't want Abel going off in the ones they'd put on him. With the wartime metal shortage, handcuffs were hard to come by. They wanted theirs back.

The FBI agents nodded. One agent went across the road to his car to get a pair he had in the trunk. The police officer on Abel's left side went with him to clear a path through the crowd while the second officer got out his keys. He unlocked Abel's handcuffs and was just turning to take the FBI cuffs when a man came running up the street.

"We got the Nazi's camp!" he yelled. "The whole place is on fire! Look there. It's going up!"

We whirled around and saw, low over the woods, a cloud of smoke funneling up into the sky. While everyone stared, a scuffle broke out near the police car and suddenly Abel was running away down the street. The officer who had unlocked his handcuffs lay sprawled on the ground. For a second, no one moved. Then somebody cried, "Get him!" and the whole crowd took off after him. The FBI agents ran across the road to their car and tried to jump in, but the people racing past blocked their way and they had to wait to get the doors open.

I was just going to take off, too, when a hand grabbed my shirt and yanked me back. It was Elliot. His eyes were wild.

"Don't," he whispered.

"Why?"

"Wait till they've gone."

"I want to go."

"He's taking them by the road. He'll cut into the woods and try to lose them. I know a short way."

"Where?"

"Come on." He led me behind the school into a dense tangle of brush and, soon, to a brook which I saw right away was the same one that went down the side of Abel's meadow. By this time of the summer, it was shallow and sluggish, and opened in front of us like a pathway through the bushes and trees. We hopped and splashed along it, climbing the bank to go around the deep places. After a while we began to smell smoke. The air got thicker and thicker until at last, through the trees, we saw flames leaping up.

Elliot stopped in his tracks. "No! Don't do that!" he yelled, and grabbed my arm. "They're burning his paintings."

"Well, let's get them out."

"They're on fire," Elliot cried. "Look, they're all on fire."

"Come on!" I said, and tried to drag him along. But his

boots wouldn't move. They stayed stuck in the stream bed.

"Elliot, come!"

He wouldn't budge.

"Elliot!"

Maybe he didn't hear me. His eyes were on the flames and he was stiff all over.

"Well, stay then!" I shouted. I pried his hand off me and ran on alone.

No one was in Abel's meadow when I came into it, but back in the woods, beyond the blaze, dark shapes were moving. Both sheds were on fire. Thick orange flames were shooting high into the air. Inside the walls, the outlines of Abel's big canvases were still visible, racked side by side down the length like trusting animals in a barn waiting for rescue. But as I watched, the end of one shed collapsed and the paintings there crumbled into fiery pieces. The flames surged higher into the air.

Maybe I went into shock myself. Back in the woods, I saw the mass of shadowy shapes move toward Abel's boat-studio, not yet touched by fire. With a shout I ran forward, madly waving my arms.

"Get away!" I shrieked. "Go back! Keep away!" They stopped, surprised, and watched me come. We faced each other over the bow of Abel's boat, and I recognized a few people, including Larry Bean from the filling station in town. They knew me, too, and in another minute would have pushed me aside and set Abel's boat on fire. But just then a loud cry rang out and Abel himself burst out of the woods.

He raced forward across the meadow, roaring with fury. He ran for one burning shed, swerved toward the other, then stopped between the two, raised his big hands to his head and began to shake it violently back and forth. A long wail rose out of his throat and trailed off below the sharp crackle of the fire. Not far from me, the men who had been stalking the boat-studio stepped back and melted away into forest shadow.

With no warning, Abel Hoffman's legs collapsed and he dropped to the ground, still holding his head. A breeze blew in off the bay. Flames leaped again in the air. A shower of sparks flew into some trees nearby and I saw how dry they were. In an instant, a small blaze flared up and glowed through the leaves.

Abel was on his feet again. He was looking over his shoulder. The crowd from the police station had begun to straggle in. Abel had led them on a roundabout route through the back woods as Elliot had said. Now they came out panting, one by one, to stare wide-eyed at the sheds. Others came up behind until a good-size throng was lined up along the far edge of the field.

Abel stood where he was and watched them come. In a little while, though, he began slowly to back away from them. He moved closer to the sheds, circled around them to the left, and came very near me. He passed by without seeing me. He was staring over his shoulder at the crowd again.

Some people had caught sight of him. They were pointing him out to a police officer.

Abel Hoffman moved away. Circling again, he gazed thoughtfully into the fire. His paintings were still visible in places. Some hadn't fallen yet. Their stretched canvas faces had burnt and split, roasting like bits of rawhide into brownish shreds. The larger frames had lasted longer and were holding their form.

Abel began to walk toward these last frames, shielding his face from the heat with his hands. He moved with steady steps, not fast and not slow. When he was almost at the fire's edge, he turned and glanced back again. Not at the crowd this time but at the world in general, it seemed to me; at the confusing green-blue, gray-brown, light-dark world he had tried to paint. He looked curiously, the way you might to catch a last glimpse of a strange place you had just finished visiting, and then he stepped into the flames. A second later, I saw the shadow of his body pass upright before a rack of paintings. Then he was gone, or in shock I shut my eyes, I can't remember which.

13

AFTERWARDS, I LOOKED for Elliot. He must have been there somewhere in the confusion of people and smoke and flying sparks but I never saw him. Only later, I went to Grandma's on my way home and found Carolyn in the backyard by herself.

"Elliot got sick," she said. "He came home and got sick in his room. Grandma heard him. Now she has to stay with him in case he does it again."

"Is he all right?"

"Grandpa gave him some medicine but he threw that up, too. He has the shivers all over."

I went up to Elliot's room and saw him curled in a knot in his bed with his eyes closed, and Grandma sitting beside him. When I went near, his eyes opened a crack and looked at me, then they closed again.

"He hasn't said a word since he came home," Grandma whispered. "Everything he has on smells of smoke. Has something happened to the painter in the woods?"

I nodded. Grandma put her finger on her lips, so we didn't talk then. Later, Elliot fell asleep and she came downstairs. I told her how Abel Hoffman had escaped from the police, and the mob had chased him until he'd walked into the flames of his own paintings. Then the wind had blown up and the fire began to spread to other parts of the field, even into the forest. Everyone was frightened and we all went to work to fight it.

For the next two hours we stamped and beat at the flames like maniacs. We cleared bushes in the fire's path, made human chains to drive back upstart blazes, wetted down branches with what water was left in the brook. Abel's boat-studio was saved, and the white-hot shed fires were contained. They burned down until all that was left were two glowing piles of charred wood. People gradually slipped off and disappeared back into the woods to go home.

Grandma covered her face with her hands and shook her head while she listened.

"That poor boy. Oh, that poor, poor boy," she said over and over. Sometimes I wasn't sure if she was talking about Elliot or Abel.

Elliot laid in bed all the rest of that day and that night. Uncle Jake sat with him, then Aunt Nan, then both of them together. The next day, he got up and seemed better. Aunt Nan stayed home from work to be sure, but he wouldn't tell her anything. He wouldn't talk to Uncle Jake, either, or to me or anyone. About mid-afternoon, he suddenly disappeared and Aunt Nan got scared that he'd run off. She started telephoning people up the road, and had all of us racing around looking for him. Grandpa even went out in the car.

A couple of hours later Elliot showed up. It turned out he hadn't been anywhere but in the barn. The whole family was furious. They thought he'd just been hiding out, taunting them, but I knew that wasn't it. I was pretty sure he'd been up in the high loft with Abel's painting, not wanting to come down the way he hadn't before. That painting was the only one left now of all those Abel had painted in the woods—a terrible thing to think about, even for me. You couldn't blame Elliot for wanting to go up there and be alone. I just hoped he wouldn't get sick all over again from being yelled at.

Everybody knew by then, because I'd told them, how he'd been spending his afternoons with Abel. They'd heard about his drawing and painting, and his trips to the post office to pick up Abel's packages. They said they were surprised that Elliot could have been that sly and secretive for so long, though I had a strange feeling Aunt Nan and Uncle Jake knew more about what he'd been doing than they let on. Grandma must have known, too, because she guessed, even before I told her, where Elliot had been the day of the fire.

Only Grandpa seemed really surprised. After supper,

when no one was looking, he spoke to Elliot, and took him out back to his office. I was worried and crept along behind to watch through the window. I got there just in time to see Grandpa crank up.

"Sneak!" he shouted at Elliot. "Liar! Fool! Did it ever occur to you that you were putting us all at risk? Running the German's errands, buying his food. Did you really suppose he would teach you to paint?"

"I guess I did," Elliot said.

"As if that would be any help to the world. The man's art was a joke, anyone could see that. You'd be better off learning to paint houses—if you could learn anything, which I'm beginning to doubt. Where's your sense, boy? Where's your self-resepct? Do you mean to go through life in this utterly mindless and irresponsible manner?"

"I hope not," Elliot said, bending low before the wind as he always did.

For that, he was let go. He knew very well how to damp down Grandpa's fury, and though part of me was glad, another part despised him for it. I knew I'd never allow myself to be put down that way. I'd have taken on the old bully if he'd said those things to me. I'd have told him where to get off and a whole lot more. So what if he hit me? I'd have laughed in his face.

The embers from the shed fires were barely cool before Sachem's Head settled back into the business of day by day wartime living: hoarding gas coupons and stretching meat-less meals, blacking out windows and painting car head-lights, buying war bonds, writing to servicemen overseas, waiting for return mail, and keeping up with troop move-ments in the newspaper.

What Abel Hoffman had done and what he deserved were questions most people didn't choose to think about very deeply or for very long. Whether this was due to shame, or shock, or a general nervousness brought on by the war, who knows, but within days of his death, Abel was buried history.

The FBI agents tried to follow up their suspicions by ransacking his boat-studio a third time. They uncovered nothing more except a supply of unopened whiskey bottles under the floorboards. With no evidence to tie Abel to any real spying activity, and the fort drawings securely attrib-uted to Elliot, who spent an hour answering questions on the score, the Feds' case was closed. The area was posted against trespassers. The studio sat abandoned under its thatched roof in the field. I walked over to visit a short time later. I was having a hard time getting the man out of my head.

"Is all his stuff still there?" Elliot asked me, casually, when I got back.

"Mostly. The FBI agents took the whiskey."

"It must still stink around there after that fire."

"It's getting better."

"Did you see Abel's hawk?"

"No. I think he's gone."

"I guess he would go."

"Maybe he got caught in the flames."

"No, he's flown off somewhere. He'll be back, I'm sure of it," Elliot said. I could see that was important to him. To tell the truth, it bolstered me up a bit, too.

"Abel's pastels are there. Do you want them?" I asked. "Someone else is going to go in there and take them if you don't."

Elliot said he didn't want them, but I guessed he might not object if they suddenly appeared. So I went over again, brought the box back and left it on the table in his room. I didn't say anything about it and he didn't either, but soon he began to use them.

My father had been missing six weeks when, with a screech of brakes, Uncle Jake arrived grim-faced in our yard one night and, two minutes later, carried my mother off in his truck. She had a telephone call up at Grandma's, a Captain Smith who, when told that Helen Saunders was at another house, asked to wait until she was brought over so he could give her his news in person.

Carolyn was tucked in for the night but not yet asleep, and I went in to be with her. For an hour we lay on her bed, staring out the window, waiting for my mother to come back.

"Is it about Daddy?" Carolyn asked.

"I don't know."

"Maybe they found him."

"Maybe," I said. She must have heard something in my voice of what I was trying not to show her, because she took hold of my hand and said:

"Don't be scared, Robby. Pretty soon we'll know."

"Who's scared?" I said, the same way Elliot always said it when he really was. That made me laugh a little. "Anyway, I guess people have a right to be scared if they're waiting for bad news about their father," I said.

She was quiet for a minute, then she asked: "People can be scared waiting for good news, too, can't they?"

I had to agree they could, but deep in my stomach a feeling was growing that this wasn't what we were going to hear. I thought of Willie Vogel, whose father had died fighting at Midway, and wondered if I would start being a bad student like him. But Willie never got very good grades, even before his father died, so it didn't seem likely.

I thought of my mother's banner with the blue star, and how she'd have to sew a new one with a gold star on it now. I wondered if we'd ever go back to the farm and if my father would come home in a box with an American flag wrapped around it like the dead servicemen I'd seen in the fort newsreels. I wondered if he'd been shot up in his plane like the navigator in his letter, or got smashed to pieces when the plane crashed. By the time Uncle Jake's headlights showed up, I'd gone through just about every way there was of being killed in a plane, and I felt weak and didn't want to look at my mother's face when she came in the front door.

So, I lay there and didn't get up. Carolyn went downstairs and when I heard my mother's voice begin to tell her something, I blocked my ears to put off hearing a little longer. Finally, my mother came up and sat on Carolyn's bed. I could see she'd been crying. When she started talking, new tears came into her eyes.

"Robert, it was your father," she said.

"I knew it," I said, my hands still over my ears.

"No, I mean on the phone. From London. He's all right."

"All right?"

"He's safe, Robert. He had a grand escape. From France. He told me all about it. Just now."

"He called?" I asked dumbly, as if I hadn't heard a word.

"Robby, are you asleep?" My mother laughed. She reached out and shook my shoulder, and I guess I had been kind of asleep for the last hour, because suddenly I felt myself rise up through a dull fog toward some surface. Then I blasted through and was wide awake, and my father was alive.

Anyone would think that the news would have caused a celebration in our house. It didn't. My mother was up early the next morning doing laundry, washing down the kitchen floor. She was going back to work the next day, she told me and Carolyn when we came downstairs.

"But, can't we bake a cake or have a party or something?" I asked. "Grandma would like to. So would Aunt Nan, I bet." The story of my father's return was so fantastic.

His plane had been shot up during a bombing run over France and lost two engines. He'd managed to fly it back as far as the English Channel, when something, maybe a gas line, had exploded and flames had erupted on board. The crew bailed out as the plane nose-dived into the sea. My father alone, unconscious and with four broken ribs from a hard landing, was rescued. By pure luck, a French fishing boat had seen his parachute hit the water and chugged over to investigate.

He was brought into port, hidden from the Germans by a French family, nursed. Finally he recovered enough to travel. Late one night, while a storm raged in the channel, he was ferried across to England in a boat so small it nearly capsized in the waves. He'd had to swim the last stretch to shore because they'd blown so far off course. A grand escape, as my mother had said. But celebrate?

My mother frowned. "Not yet," she said. "Your father's not home yet. We'll wait till he's here to start waving our flags."

I saw something more than superstition in this answer, and it made me angry. "Dad will never come here so we might as well give up ever waving anything," I said in disgust.

"What do you mean?"

"Captain Smith? Dad couldn't say who he was when he called his own family? After he was lost and almost died?"

"He wanted to talk to me first is all," my mother said. "He told me to tell everyone he was all right, and I did, last night. Now Robert, that's the end of it. Don't say anymore about celebrations to Grandma or Nan, because we're all doing fine here, just fine. We'll leave everything the way it is, that's my final word."

And so our old routine started up again. Carolyn still spent the day with Grandma. I worked odd jobs around the two houses and in the vegetable gardens which, along with the eggs from Grandma's hens, we depended on more and more for our meals. At night, we ate with Uncle Jake and Elliot, then stayed on until my mother got back, when we walked home to our cottage. In this way, we passed through September. School loomed. Carolyn was to enter the first grade, and she felt nervous about it.

"Why do you have to work so much?" she blurted out to my mother one evening on the way home. "I'm sick of Grandma. She never lets me to do anything."

"I work to pay for our food and rent," my mother said. Maybe she was more tired than usual, because she added, "We're a working family, Carolyn, in case you forgot. I work. Your brother works. Your father works in the war. Your job is staying with Grandma, not a great deal to ask, considering."

"Yes it is a great deal," Carolyn said.

"You don't know how lucky you are," snapped my mother who, having grown up as an orphan in other people's houses, had no patience for those who could "carry on in a coat closet" (as she often said) if things didn't go their way. This especially applied to her children.

"Wait a minute," I said, "doesn't Grandpa own our cottage? Grandma says he does."

"Yes, he does," my mother answered. "He bought it back from the bank after Uncle Jake lost his mortgage. That's who I pay rent to."

"Why doesn't he just let us live there if he owns it? He's got enough money."

"Because your grandfather believes in people paying their own way. And so do I," my mother said.

"Even family?" I asked.

"Even family. He's a hard man, but fair." That raised a question I'd been wanting to ask for some time.

"Was it fair when Grandpa sat by while Uncle Jake and Aunt Nan lost their house? He could have helped them," I said. "Most people would if they saw their own children in trouble."

My mother made no answer to this. When I glanced over to see why not, I saw she had turned her face away toward the sun, just then dipping below the horizon.

"Well, I don't think fairness came into it," I told her. "I think Grandpa wanted to punish Uncle Jake and Aunt Nan. Grandpa thinks people should be taught a lesson if they don't do the right thing. He gets angry and then he does something to teach them."

"Maybe they need to be taught a lesson," my mother said. "Maybe they'll be better for it."

"Was Dad taught a lesson?" I asked her. "Was he better for it? Is that why he went away and never came back?"

As if she had not heard me, my mother strode ahead to catch up with my sister.

No one could say Grandpa didn't work hard. More often than not, he was out in the evenings, making house calls, running up to the hospital. Being a doctor, he had extra gas rationing coupons, and he was generous about visiting patients who weren't able to come to him.

That was just fine with us. Everyone felt relieved when he wasn't at the table. Grandma could make a joke without being glared at. Uncle Jake and Elliot could act like their real selves. There was even a chance the conversation might swing around to something interesting, like my father.

We all wanted to talk about him, I think. His name had been outlawed for so long. Now, with his incredible return, everyone was thinking of him and, at the supper table, behind Grandpa's back, we began for the first time to speak about him as a family.

I remember Elliot asking my mother when "Uncle Ken" would be coming home. My mother had no idea and, as it happened, my father wouldn't take a leave for another five months, but that simple question, posed so openly, gave me a shock of relief I'll never forget.

Another time, Uncle Jake told about a prank he and my dad had pulled off as kids. They'd imitated Grandma's voice over the telephone ("Hello? This is Mrs. Saunders down on Parson's Lane . . .") and ordered a gallon container of store ice cream delivered to the end of the driveway.

"When it came, we told the man to put it on the house bill and ate it on the spot. No one ever knew," Uncle Jake said, with a big grin at Grandma. He and my father were exactly the same age, it turned out. They'd been in the same class at school.

Grandma kind of cocked her head. "And who says no one ever knew?"

Uncle Jake stopped smiling. "Well, no one ever said they knew."

"Let the record show that the day was a hot one and that, by good fortune, you boys had a secret ally in the house," Grandma said. "But don't try it again or I won't be responsible for what happens." She shook her finger at Uncle Jake and glanced back over her shoulder, as if Grandpa's glowering face were about to appear. We all broke up laughing.

On other evenings there were other stories, about how my dad read everything on the early aviators and wanted nothing but to fly. Aunt Nan remembered him as a teenager sneaking out of school, trying to build glider planes in the woods.

"He'd launch them off the bluffs at Windmill Hill, but they never worked. He had crash after crash! It's a wonder he didn't kill himself."

"I guess he was determined, because he went on to be a pilot," I said.

"Against his father's wishes," Uncle Jake said. I saw Grandma's hands press suddenly against the table. The next second, she put an end to the stories by ordering the table cleared for dessert. There was still a line, I saw, beyond which we must not go when we talked about my father.

The night I heard about Dad's glider planes, I followed Elliot up to his room after dinner, thinking I might somehow get him to tell me more. By then, it was mid-September. As it had in Ohio, school began later here, where farm kids were needed to help out with the fall harvest, so we still had a little time left before classes started.

"What are you drawing these days?" I began by asking.

He showed me some pencil sketches of the table in his room with stuff on it, of his bed and the light bulb hanging down, of his shoes, the back of his door, somebody's hand in close-up held before a window. All indoor scenes, really personal.

"Whose hand is that?"

"Mine."

He'd used Abel's pastels to color the sketches in and they were good. Like photos almost, they were so true to life. He'd gone back to real drawing, I was glad to see. Elliot didn't look happy with them, though. He hadn't looked happy about anything he'd done since Abel's fire.

"Tried any more of the ocean?" I asked.

"No."

"Just as well."

He sat silent, fingering a pencil.

"That was pretty amazing what your mother said about my dad," I said, "that he wanted to be a flyer, even way back. I wish I could've known him then."

Elliot nodded.

"Grandma has a picture of him from when he was about our age. He's holding a gun and his leg is still okay. She said he liked to hunt. He looks pretty normal."

Elliot shrugged.

"So, what happened?" I asked.

"What do you mean?"

"Why did he have to leave?"

"How should I know?" Elliot said.

"I think you do."

"How could I? It was before I was born."

"I know, but . . ."

Elliot shook his head. He leaned forward and ran off a sketch of an army Jeep. He got the headlights and windshield just right. From the front, army Jeeps have a kind of dopey expression. He got that, too.

"I saw one of these today. It came around the corner and ran over the McGowan's dog," he said. He bent and drew a dead dog beside the Jeep. Then he colored the dog in, reddish tan, with one of Abel's pastels. "You know which dog I mean?"

I knew. "Too bad. I liked that old mutt. He used to follow me around sometimes," I said.

"He was hungry," Elliot said. "He was asking for food. The McGowans didn't feed him right."

"How do you know?"

"I watched him."

"You should have said something."

"What good would that have done?"

Elliot laid the sharp edge of his ruler down and tore the Jeep picture angrily off the roll.

He put it aside and unrolled a longer piece of store wrap. He lined the ruler up, tore the long sheet off the roll, and anchored the corners with four flat stones he'd taken from the beach. It was a method he had and I'd seen him do it before.

"Know where Grandpa keeps his guns?" he asked.

I didn't.

Elliot bent and began to draw. "There's a closet behind the dining room door. Inside is a gun rack. He has three guns, two kinds of shotgun and a twenty-two."

"Must be one of the shotguns my father's holding in the photo Grandma has."

"Probably is."

"I guess Grandpa doesn't do much shooting anymore."

"He doesn't do any shooting," Elliot said, sketching away on one edge of the paper. He had drawn the closet with its door open to show the gun rack. The two shotguns were in the rack; the twenty-two was missing.

"Grandma said my father was a good shot," I said. "Grandpa taught him. He had a dog named Baron. They used to go off hunting together and bring home stuff for dinner. Grouse and rabbits and things. One time, he shot a thirty-pound wild turkey and they had it for Christmas dinner."

Elliot didn't answer. He was drawing on the other edge of the paper now, sketching in the kitchen, the kitchen door, which was swung open. There was some space beyond the door that was probably going to be the backyard. He left that part empty for now. The way he was drawing this picture was different from anything I'd seen him do before. It was as if the house was sliced open. You could see the outside of the house, the yard and front door, but you could also see inside two rooms, the dining room and the kitchen.

"What are you drawing, El?" I asked, but he wouldn't answer.

He drew Grandma's stove in the kitchen, a china cabinet that stands against the wall in the dining room, the kitchen sink and the icebox, part of the dining room table and some chairs. He went back and forth between the two rooms, filling them in, and soon I saw that in a space between the rooms, he was drawing a person.

"Is that Grandpa?" I asked him.

Elliot looked up at me. He raised a finger to his lips,

then went on drawing, his eyes carefully following the point of his pencil.

I knew it was Grandpa from the round shape of his head. He looked younger, though, had more hair and wasn't wearing his glasses. He was in profile, staring into the kitchen, and his arms were lifted in front of him. He was holding something up before his face. What was it? Elliot moved on without sketching it in. He worked on the space beyond the kitchen door.

It was the backyard, as I thought. Grandma's herb garden appeared. Her big tin watering can. She'd forget it sometimes, run off to do something else. I began to see how this picture was sort of like a story unfolding.

"Who is that?"

Elliot had begun to draw another person, not Grandma. It was a young man with dark hair and an angry face. He looked at first to be walking away, but then it seemed that he had stumbled or fallen down. His body was at a strange angle to his legs.

"Elliot, please tell me what's happening here?"

Elliot's lips were pressed shut. He would never tell.

"Elliot!" I stared over his shoulder at the drawing coming to life on the long piece of store wrap.

He was working on Grandpa. Grandpa had a gun. It was the twenty-two. He was sighting along the barrel, standing in the little hall, aiming through the kitchen, out the kitchen door. He was pulling the trigger. The gun was going off. The young man was falling. His leg was gushing blood.

"Is that my father? Elliot, is it?"

With Abel Hoffman's pastels, Elliot put in the yellow of Grandpa's shirt, and the flesh color of his hands and face. He made the kitchen walls light blue, the way they are, and the sink and icebox white. Outside, he made the grass green, the trees brown with green leaves, the field a soft wheat color. Then he put in the red, a big pool of it, beside Grandma's pretty herb garden.

14

EVERYONE HAD BEEN in the house, after all: Aunt Nan and Uncle Jake, already keeping company with each other; Grandma, though she insisted that she never heard the fight or the gun going off. ("Which is strange," my mother commented, later. "She was bound to be nearby.")

They'd argued over a job, another of the many arguments they were having at that time. They seemed opposed on every issue. For several years they'd been at cross-purposes, Grandpa driving my father to achieve along well-beaten tracks; my father backing off, choosing paths of his own. That spring, as his graduation from high school approached and then took place, the arguments grew worse.

My father refused to apply to college. Not yet, he said. He wasn't ready. He wanted to work at an airfield on Long Island, get his pilot's license and fly for the U. S. Postal Service, which was just then expanding routes all over the country. After that, he'd decide. He needed time to think things through.

Grandpa was furious. Flying was a madman's game. He knew what was best. My father should go into medicine, become a doctor, aim for the things in life that were of known value, which had already been achieved by Grandpa, no less, and proven solid.

Freeloader, he called my father. Imbecile. Ungrateful jackass. After everything my father had taken from the family, been given free and lovingly—education, respect, good health, care, and support—did a son owe a father nothing? *Nothing?*

A day came in June when my father announced that he'd had enough. He was leaving, he said, that very afternoon, would hitchhike if he had to, to catch the ferry at Point Judith.

When Grandpa saw that my father was packed and ready to leave, that he'd asked his own mother for a ride across the bridge, that he would not discuss it anymore, yelled insults, used filthy language, turned his back and walked away when he was being spoken to; when Grandpa saw that he would not win this battle either, after all the others lost, after watching, day by day, the disintegration of his fine, trusted boy (a crack shot at twelve!) into this angry, foul-mouthed young man; after Grandpa had stood it and more, after he'd tried everything—arguing, reasoning, patience, discipline—and nothing had worked and there was nothing else to do but watch my father leave for who knew what life of waste and ruination, after this . . .

He could not remember pulling the trigger, Aunt Nan told us.

"He denied it to your grandmother and to himself. The gun went off in his hands, he said. He would not take responsibility, could not believe what he had done. I saw him, though," she said. "He was aiming through the door. Jake and I were in the dining room. We saw the whole thing."

The bullet struck my father's right leg, smashing the bone above his knee. He was facing the open kitchen door when he fell, and he lay on the grass by the herb garden without a cry or a word. He watched as his father leaned the gun against the kitchen wall and walked out to help him.

My grandfather made a tourniquet from his own cotton shirt. He left Aunt Nan to hold it firm while he went for morphine, antiseptic, his surgery tools. With help from Uncle Jake, they moved my father a few feet into the shade and Grandpa operated right there to remove the bullet.

The bone was badly fractured. He brought the pieces together the best he could for the moment. Splinted the thigh. Carried my father indoors to the guest room bed, where my father lay groggy and suffering, eating nothing, speaking to no one. Grandpa had planned to take him to a hospital the next day, but that night, despite the morphine, my father carried out a plan of his own.

Coming into the room to help him to the bathroom the next morning, Grandma found his bed empty. The crutches, which he'd not yet been able to use, were gone.

Somehow, he'd dressed, dragged himself outside to the family car, and driven off, a feat which must have caused him excruciating pain.

He took the early morning train from Riverton to Providence, that much was reported. Where he went next to hide and nurse himself, he never told. He disappeared and, though Grandma waited every day to hear from him, he never called, not in the weeks after, or the months. Three years went by before a printed card arrived from Ohio telling of his marriage to my mother. A year later he wrote personally to announce, with obvious pride, the day and hour of my birth.

All this, we learned from Aunt Nan. I went straight to my mother the night of Elliot's drawing. I told her everything, and armed with the right questions, we extracted the rest of the story the next morning. In whispers. Out of Grandma's hearing.

"Don't speak to her about it. She believes it was an accident," Aunt Nan warned.

"How could she?" my mother asked.

"I think she must. It would kill her otherwise. It would kill them both."

"How did Elliot find out?" I wanted to know.

"Jake and I told him," Aunt Nan said, "for his own good. We were moving here, you see. Your father thought he should know."

"My father?" I asked.

Aunt Nan nodded. "He was afraid for Elliot. He said he should be warned about Grandpa's temper."

"His temper!" I cried in disgust. "Is that what you call it?"

"Hush, Robert," my aunt said. "Please, not so loud." She lay her finger against my lips to shut them.

My father never came to see us in Sachem's Head. Five months later, my mother, Carolyn and I took a train down to meet him in Washington, D.C., where he'd gone on a two-week leave. We stayed in a hotel, climbed the National Monument, saw the Capitol, ate at restaurants, and took pictures of ourselves under the cherry blossoms.

Dad looked thinner. He wore a metal brace on his back under his shirt, and his dark hair had gray in it, but we didn't mention these changes. We knew that, like his limp, they weren't meant to be noticed. When Carolyn wanted a piggyback ride one time, my mother snapped at her and told her it was time to grow up and walk on her own two feet. I could see she was protecting my father after all he'd been through, and I didn't blame her. I was being pretty careful of him myself. I never once asked him about Sachem's Head or his life there. I wanted to. I was desperate to know his side of things, but I kept quiet, and he volunteered nothing. As far as I know, the subject of Grandpa never came up.

Elliot came up, though. My father wanted to know about him.

I told him about Elliot's amazing drawing, how he'd kept it a secret from everyone. I told how Abel Hoffman had been in the art book my father sent, and all about Elliot's trips to the woods. I described the big guns and Abel's arrests, and how stupid Elliot had been to keep going back to him when the whole town was watching.

Finally, I told about Abel's terrible walk into the fire that had shocked everybody, whatever side they were on, and made them want to forget Abel and everything that had happened. Dad nodded, as if it didn't surprise him. He said that kind of forgetfulness was something he'd seen in human nature before.

"Is Elliot still drawing?" he asked.

I said he was, as secretively as ever. Like everyone else, he never talked about Abel but I knew he thought about him because he was always up in the loft with Abel's painting.

"Elliot keeps saying he wants to meet you," I told my father. "He's hoping you'll come visit. Can't you? On your next leave? It would really mean a lot to him."

Dad didn't answer for a while. He was so quiet I thought he might never answer, but finally he said, "You tell Elliot to come visit the farm. Tell him he can come stay with us after we settle back there, look into art school in Cincinnati if he wants. He'll need to get out of Sachem's Head if he's going to do something with his talent. He'll need to get away before it's too late."

It was as close as he'd go to telling me what had happened

to him back there when he was a kid. Whatever his reasons were, I knew he probably wasn't ever going to say much more.

"What about you? Are you doing all right? he asked me. When I said I was, he gave me a quick look.

"Well watch yourself," he said. "You watch yourself, Robert."

When my father's leave was up, we all said good-bye at the railroad station. He caught a train down the coast to a ship that was heading for England. We took the train back to Sachem's Head. Somehow my mother had convinced him that we were better off staying there for the time being, even knowing what we all did about Grandpa.

As soon as we got home, I told Elliot what my father had said about coming to live with us. It made him pretty happy. I think he would have left right then if he could have. As it was, he got out a year later, in the spring of 1944, when my father came home for good and we moved back to the farm.

Elliot lived with us during his high-school years. Aunt Nan and Uncle Jake said it was the best thing for him until they could get their own house. By the time they did, he'd been accepted at an art school in Chicago and gone off to study. He's set up his own life there now, got an apartment downtown, a lot of nutty friends in the art world. I'm a college senior myself, headed toward medical school of all things, but I take the train up to see him a couple of times a year, or he comes down to Ohio. He loves the farm, just like

I do—the wide sky passing high overhead, the fields sweeping in from all sides. "Wing room" my dad still calls the feeling you get out there. Elliot knows what he means. It means he can paint right out in the open, whatever he wants, without anyone trying to stop him. He can leave and go back to Chicago, or any other place in the world, whenever he decides to, no questions asked.

The last time I went to visit him, I saw he'd persuaded Aunt Nan to send him Abel's bomb painting. It must have been up in that loft for nine years or more, but it still looked all right. More than all right, actually. It's a knockout. Elliot was right about Abel. The guy was brilliant. He's beginning to get recognized again in Europe, where a lot of his work survived the war after all.

Apparently this painting Elliot has is worth a mint because it was the last one Abel did. Elliot's friends in Chicago kid him about becoming a millionaire and retiring to the South Pacific. Some offers have come in from museums, but Elliot would never sell it. He still has his birds'-egg collection, too, still keeps it under his bed, and anybody who knows him knows that nothing, absolutely nothing, will ever make him give it up.

Elliot says I'm slowly getting brought up-to-date in my taste for modern art, emphasis on the slowly. I think I still have a way to go because the paintings Elliot does get wilder every time I look. He's always trying different styles and ideas. Usually, I hate them at first. Then I kind of warm up to them. One thing is, you can see he isn't leaving himself out of his pictures anymore, the way he used to. He's in them one hundred percent now, showing his feelings, giving people his own crazy views. Less perfectness, Abel said. More you-ness. Well, that's pretty much what Elliot's doing. He's selling the stuff, too. Making a name for himself. Sometimes, I stand back and look at him in wonder and think, "Where is this screwball headed next?"

There was one other discovery I made during our time in Rhode Island. One evening, about a week after we returned from seeing my father in Washington, my mother called Grandma from the road to say that she and Aunt Nan were broken down in Portsmouth on the way home. She'd started going to work in Newport again. Carolyn and I were back in school. These kinds of breakdowns had happened before. The car was old. Parts were hard to come by. At such times, Carolyn and I bedded down at Grandma's for the night while Uncle Jake went to pick up the women and deal with the problem.

I'd be given a blanket and pillow and told to stay up in Elliot's attic. Usually, I'd sleep beside his bed so we could talk. But that night I didn't want to. I was thinking about Dad, hoping he'd be okay. I wished he'd write me when he got to England but I knew he probably wouldn't. He'd be too busy. It seemed I never could get as close to him as I wanted, and that kind of depressed me. I lay down by myself under some low rafters, where I could look up through a skylight and see the moon. In the distance, I heard an air-raid siren go off, and afterwards the rumble of a navy flight squadron passing by high up, heading out to sea. Both were such familiar sounds by then that I was glad to hear them, and felt a little peace come into me.

It's a comfortable feeling to know you're being guarded while you sleep, that your enemies are well-watched and kept at a distance. Not since mid-August had the Germans torpedoed a ship off our coast. The big guns were in place, ready to shoot if need be, but a new confidence was rising in town, an awareness that the ocean was wide and difficult to cross, that our enemy had begun to draw back, that the war would be fought there, in far-off Europe, and not here on our Rhode Island beaches.

That night, though, as the roar of airplanes faded into the distance, the sound of another motor rose in my ear. Down the driveway it came, and I knew from the way the motor turned off, with a little cough, that it was Grandpa's car.

He was coming home late from a visit to a patient. I heard the car door slam, the crunch of his feet on the gravel. I heard his heavy footsteps as he came toward the house, and the slap of his soles on the stone steps going up to the front door. Elliot must have heard him, too, because he rolled over quickly and lay still. We both listened to the front door open and shut, to the muffled tread of Grandpa's progress through the house.

A little flame of anger sprang up in me when I heard him get to the kitchen. I thought of what he'd done to my father there, how he still hadn't owned up to it but went on hiding like a coward and bullying the people around him. It struck me how your enemy can be someone who lives close to you, where you're most vulnerable, not just on the other side of an ocean. The flame blazed. I got hotter and angrier. I wanted to get up right then and do something. I wanted to fight him.

The fire began to go sideways. Lying there in bed, I got angry at Grandma for pretending not to know what she really did know all these years. And at Aunt Nan for covering up; at Uncle Jake for being a weakling and not standing up to Grandpa when somebody needed to stop him. My mother wasn't much better, the way she hid her true feelings from us and wouldn't talk about things that upset her.

Elliot must have heard me wrestling around with all this because suddenly he spoke.

"Don't let it bother you," he said. "That's the trick."

"What trick?"

"The one that works against everything."

"Well it does bother me. I can't help it."

"You can help it," Elliot said. "You've just got to figure out how."

He rolled over and was quiet. Five minutes later, I knew from the sound of his breathing that he'd fallen asleep.

I lay awake for most of that night trying to think of

how I could go on living in a family that had so much wrong with it. I thought of the secrets we couldn't speak about, the wounds that would never be fixed, the people who would go on pretending that things were normal and honest when nothing was, when it was all lies and covering up and hiding your real feelings.

I was still awake at 5:30 A.M. when another squadron of reconnaissance planes roared back toward the base at Quonset. I tried to catch sight of them through the skylight but they passed by. Then, as the sky brightened outside, I saw something carved into the beam near the skylight over my head. I got up to look. There were my father's initials— K.B.S.—carved deep and black into the wood. I couldn't believe it at first. I ran my finger over them a few times to make sure it was really true.

I wanted to wake up Elliot to show him, but he was sound asleep and looked too peaceful to disturb.

So I lay back down to wait for morning, when I could ask Aunt Nan or someone how the initials might have come to be there. Maybe my father had slept here, too, so he could see the moon like me. Maybe this was his room. Or maybe he just liked to come here to be alone.

I guess I must have finally dozed off while I was waiting because suddenly a little silver plane was flying toward me and I was back in the dream that had been bothering me ever since we came to Sachem's Head.

I saw the plane's wings flash in the sun and heard the

throb of the motor come closer and closer. Inside the cockpit, the shadowy form of the pilot was there, but I couldn't
see his face again.

This time, I remembered Elliot's advice. I thought if I
could just shout loud enough, really loud, the man in the
pilot's seat might hear me. So I yelled, "Turn your head!"
Then, with all my might, I bellowed, "Show me who you
are!"

After this, a hand grabbed my shoulder and I was
shaken so hard my eyes flew open. There was Elliot laughing down at me and I was back in the real world with the
sun of a new day pouring into my face.

The Art of Keeping Cool by Janet Taylor Lisle

Literature Circle Questions

Use the questions and activities that follow to get more out of the experience of reading *The Art of Keeping Cool* by Janet Taylor Lisle.

1.   At the beginning of the story, Robert sees big naval guns being hauled through town on their way to Fort Brooks. What do those tools of war look and sound like?

2.   Why did Robert, his mother, and his sister move from their farm in Ohio to the Saunders' house in Rhode Island?

3.   For most of the story, Robert's father lives overseas. Where is Robert's father, and what is he doing there?

4.   The author uses many idioms in the narration and dialogue of the story, such as: "They threw a man in jail so he could 'cool his heels,'" and "He could be 'a real pain in the neck.'" Some idioms were more common during the 1940s than they are today. Select an idiom from the book and explain to your group its literal and figurative meanings.

5.   Near the end of the story, when Robert is older, he thinks about mistakes made by members of his family. He is struck by "how your enemy can be someone who lives close to you, where you're most vulnerable, not just on the other side of an ocean." What does Robert mean by that?

Note: The following questions are keyed to Bloom's Taxonomy: Knowledge: 1-3;
Comprehension: 4-5; Application 6-9; Analysis 10; Synthesis: 11; Evaluation 12-13.

6. What kinds of resources—such as books, maps, and interviews—did the author probably use to write the historically-accurate parts of this book? Why would these have been vital to her work?

7. Toward the end of the book, Elliott says: "Everything that happened to [Abel] in Germany is happening all over again here [in America]." What examples can you find in the story to prove that this is true?

8. Though the fighting takes place mainly overseas, the events of World War II strongly affect the lives of each character in the book. Select one of the main characters. Provide examples of how that person's life is changed due to America's involvement in the war.

9. The story takes place in 1942, when rapid means of communication, such as email, do not exist. How would events in Robert's life have differed if email had been available?

10. Near the end of *The Art of Keeping Cool*, Abel Hoffman reacts without thinking to the burning of his paintings with a terrible result. Why do you think he acted this way? What else could he have done?

11. Do you agree with the actions of the police in Rhode Island when they arrest Abel Hoffman for the submarine attack? Give reasons for your answers.

12. The townspeople suspect Abel of being a spy for the Germans, in part because he has a German accent and is a recluse. Do you think their reasons are justified? Why or why not?

13. For many years, Robert believes that his father's limp was caused by a plane crash years ago. Describe the incident that actually caused the man's "bad leg." How would you have handled that incident, had you been Grandpa?

Activities

Based on descriptions in the book, make a map of the local Rhode Island setting, including Robert's home in his grandparents' house; the village at Sachem's Head, Fort Brooks; Abel's hidden home in the woods; etc. Use the map as a visual aid as you retell the story.

Create an article for a local Rhode Island paper in 1942 describing one effect of World War II on the people of Sachem's Head. Examples: the arrival of big guns at Fort Brooks, the death of a soldier overseas, the growing trend of housewives working in factories.